A Certain Time, A Certain Place

Teresa Francis

If you could time travel to another era, would you ?

Published in Australia by Sid Harta Books & Print Pty Ltd,
ABN: 34632585293
23 Stirling Crescent, Glen Waverley, Victoria 3150 Australia
Telephone: +61 3 9560 9920, Facsimile: +61 3 9545 1742
E-mail: author@sidharta.com.au

First published in Australia 2023
This edition published 2023
Copyright © Teresa Francis 2023
Cover design, typesetting: WorkingType (www.workingtype.com.au)

Teresa Francis
A Certain Time, A Certain Place
ISBN: 978-1-922958-35-8
pp198

About the author

Office work was my life's profession, and I am now retired. I love writing and have done so all my life. Writing *A Certain Time, A Certain Place* was most enjoyable; I trust that my readers will also enjoy the novel.

In memory of John

Brother, advisor and protector

Acknowledgements

Many thanks to Gill and Geoff,

friends who encouraged me.

Contents

Chapter 1

DANIEL WESLEY

It was the day she would lose her husband, but she didn't know it. Daniel smiled up at Laura, his wife of two years, as she came to the kitchen bench and handed him a steaming cup of coffee. She was beautiful, her chestnut hair and big brown eyes were enticing. He thought back to when he had married her; he had not been in love with her, but these days, wow!

She put her arms around his neck and kissed the top of his head. She could smell Apple Blossom shampoo. He traced her hand with his fingers.

'I'm going to take the car to Benson's Motors; I need help with the alternator.' He smiled at her.

Laura gazed into his big brown eyes. He was half Greek, half Australian and had the dark features of a Greek, although he was no god.

Yes, he was tall and dark, but not really handsome. But to Laura he was everything: her Dan, her lover, her husband.

She waved to him as he got into their old but reliable Volvo, and he smiled that 'my teeth are whiter than anyone's' smile. She would never see him again.

Three hours later his business partner Jeremy Tate was standing on the front doorstep with an anxious-looking policeman in tow.

Jeremy, blond hair in his eyes and the power of speech betrayed, was as white as a ghost and moving from one foot to the other.

The solemn-looking policeman asked, 'Are you the wife of Daniel Wesley?'

Laura would remember the words forever. The words that stripped her life of happiness. Dan had been in a car accident, and he died at the scene. Daniel Wesley, twenty-eight years old, married, with a brilliant future, gone in an instant.

That was the day her life became melancholy. Strange word, melancholy, but apt, definitely perfect to describe her life without her husband, that darling man, the Mr Fix-It of her life. 'Leave it to me, Darling, don't worry, I'll do it,' all gone.

When a person dies, all sorts of other things die;

the conversations, the laughter. In their place seeps an overwhelming silence, gloom.

Then, in the morning when eyes are open, the thought hits like a sledgehammer, *he isn't here*.

No rush now to get ready and out the door early in the morning. His eager question, loving and true, 'I'll see if I can pick you up for lunch, are you free today, Laura?'

Then he would ask, 'Can you be a sweetheart and pick up my dry-cleaning? No problem if you're too busy.'

Laura, busy or not, could never refuse him anything. Being an orphan with absolutely no family, he was all she had.

It was not the love she had expected, it was not ultra-passionate, it was Dan and Laura – married couple. Dan was an architect, trying to start his own company with Jeremy.

Laura worked for an insurance company. She sat in a row of anonymous workstations, an uninteresting nine-to-five job.

Then there was the funeral. If Laura was to remember one thing about that day, it would be the relentless rain. It was dismal and bleak; fitting for the task of burying a man that she wasn't sure she could live without.

For the next seven weeks, Laura was in a daze, trying to sleep, trying to function at all. There were things she needed to attend to, although she did not have to tackle his business. Jeremy was winding it up, not wanting to continue without Dan.

'Besides,' he had said, 'Dan was the architectural brain, I'm the entrepreneur. I was going to bring him the contracts, office blocks, hospitals, railway stations.' He scoffed, 'Now—' he trailed off.

Dan had life insurance, Laura too. But she wasn't sure where the policies were. She laughed then. She was in insurance, but didn't know where the policies were? Pathetic, she told herself sarcastically.

She would think of things she must do but had no strength of will or energy to do them. Tomorrow, she would promise, but as the saying goes, tomorrow never comes.

Then on a Thursday morning, the surprises just kept coming.

That morning she watched the two police officers make their way back to their car, dodging the rain and hanging on to their hats. They had come to explain that the accident would be going to court. Laura felt emotional. The investigator had finalised his report, and a certain Edward Richards had been charged with vehicular homicide.

He had been high on drugs, and also drunk, his state almost certainly causing Dan's death. Someone being charged seemed to give her some sort of peace. She sighed.

After the police left, Jeremy came, and with a very worried face sat drinking tea with her at the kitchen bench. At first, he would look at her, and then look away, anxious.

She had no energy to ask him what was wrong. It must be something to do with their business. How wrong she had been.

'There's something I have to tell you about Dan.'

Laura put her cup down.

'I thought I could keep it to myself, but it's been bothering me.'

'Okay,' Laura said. She looked at him expectantly.

'When Dan first met you, he—' Jeremy trailed off then seemed to straighten up, 'he did not love you, but he wanted to marry you.'

Laura was puzzled.

'He had a plan. To insure your life and then have you meet with an accident and he would collect.'

Laura had heard the words, but it was difficult to comprehend.

Finally, she said, 'No,' in a very soft voice, then louder, 'No!'

Jeremy stood up abruptly and began to babble. 'I'm sorry, I thought you should know. He didn't love you when you married, but then I saw that he did love you and that I didn't need to warn you, he wasn't going to—' he hesitated, 'do anything.'

Laura put her hand over her mouth, she could hardly breathe, and her heart was beating so fast.

Later she sat at the dining room table with wedding photos. When you love someone and they love you, don't you know? The wedding was lovely, the honeymoon was happy. So happy! And yet, today Jeremy had told her it was all a lie!

She did not think Dan capable of murder. However, he had planned to murder her. It seemed so preposterous. And yet, although Jeremy could have kept this to himself, he had told her that the man she had married she did not know.

She sat in the dark, so devastated, so very broken. She cried and cried until there were no more tears left. She fell, exhausted, onto their bed, fully clothed and defeated. She slept.

Later that week, she got a call from Jeremy; he wanted to take her out to lunch. She had not showered in days. She had quit her job by phone and sat mindlessly in front of the TV, hour after hour, until it grew dark and she would get into bed. She hated that part of the evening. Dan's clothes hung in the walk-in robe. His smell was still there; his brown Oxfords were sitting in the shoe rack, next to hers. He had joked, 'You have nineteen pairs of shoes, Laura, I have five. I may have to take out a loan if you go on like this.' She had laughed and punched him playfully. He had hugged her to him and she felt loved, safe. Was it really all a lie?

She showered, washed her hair. Styled it and piled it up on top of her head, securing it with a plastic hair clip. She wore a long, black skirt and a white blouse, with black patent shoes. She managed to put on makeup and jewellery, although she hesitated to put her engagement and wedding rings on. She had thrown them in her jewellery box and had stopped wearing them. She had to face up to the fact that she had been betrayed. He had not loved her, and yet, she was sure that there was love there. In his eyes; in the way she caught him staring at her with a smile.

Laura was taken to a secluded venue on Little Abbott Street. It was one of those fashionable teashops that Melbourne society raves about. Conversation was difficult, but Jeremy was making a great effort. Yes, she had resigned, no, she hadn't thought about what to do now and, yes, she still did not drink alcohol.

'I want you to consider something for me.'

What now, she thought.

'I know Malcolm Johnson; you know, the professor?' Jeremy said.

'That guy who works for the hospital.'

'Yes,' said Jeremy enthusiastically, pleased that she knew of him.

'The North Western Hospital, he is trying to raise funds for their new wing. It is in need of money and—'

Laura touched his arm. 'Jeremy, I am not going to voluntarily call people and ask for donations.'

'No, no,' he said, 'nothing like that.'

'Well, what then?' Laura said, slightly annoyed.

'The professor fell down some stairs and is in a wheelchair. He needs help.'

'That's what the NDIS is for,' Laura said, again annoyed.

'Laura, will you listen to me, please!'

She was taken aback. She just nodded.

'The professor has a team of people who do volunteer work to raise funds for the hospital. He is, however, working on a pet project of his.'

'He needs someone to help with that. You are a very fast typist, skilled at office work, I thought you could help him out for a while, perhaps it would get you out of the house, take your mind off things.' He looked up expectantly at her.

'What would I have to do, type?' It sounded a bit odd.

'I'm not sure; you need to see him, ask him. Any sort of help you could offer would be appreciated, I'm sure.'

Laura thought about it. 'Well,' she said, 'I suppose I could talk to him, see what he needs.'

'Excellent,' said Jeremy, smiling.

'Now, what would you like to order?'

Chapter 2

THE PROFESSOR

On a bright Wednesday afternoon, Laura made her way to the professor's home in Parkville. He had given her his address on the phone. The professor's home was a beautiful double-storied terrace, obviously well over a hundred years old. There were red-painted wrought iron banisters and huge windows. Laura just knew it was National Trust. She went up the tiled path and rang an antique doorbell by the large, imposing front door.

After some time, the door creaked open very slowly. The professor, in a wheelchair that seemed a bit small for him, was a slim man dressed in a grey suit. He had white hair at the sides and none on top. His eyes were kindly, and he smiled widely.

'Laura, it is Laura?'

'Yes.'

'Oh, come in, come in, I have so wanted to meet you. Let's

have some tea and a little chat.' He began to laugh. 'I'm not sure you will want to work with me, but,' he pointed a finger at her, 'we shall see.'

Laura sat on a large, soft, cream-coloured sofa. It was very comfortable. In front of her was an antique Victorian coffee table. By the window was a majestic, black, grand piano.

As the professor went to prepare the tea, Laura sat down at the piano and played, it had a beautiful tone. She noticed a photo on the wall of a lovely woman smiling. She knew from Jeremy that the professor was a widower, and assumed the photo was of his late wife.

The professor wheeled himself back into the room with a tray on his lap, and Laura rushed to assist him. Eventually they sat down to have their tea. A floral teapot took centre stage with matching tea cups and saucers. A plate of shortbread biscuits lay on a small silver platter.

'I know you are going to be shocked, well,' he nodded quickly, 'surprised, at least, at what I am about to say.'

Laura was intrigued.

'I wonder if you have ever thought of the power of one's mind.'

'You mean like meditation?'

'Yes, but deeper than that.'

'I once learnt to hypnotise myself so that I could stop

smoking,' said Laura.

She did not mention that she had also used it to stop drinking alcohol. Two years before she met Dan she gave up alcohol entirely and changed her life. Her drinking sessions with her friend Diane had become a concern. Dan was very proud of her when she told him. She felt sad at the memory of him, of how encouraging he had been.

The professor continued, 'Good, good, you may understand what I am about to say next. I have stumbled on, invented, whatever you care to choose, a certain process of using your mind in a very fascinating way!' He was excited, and his eyes seemed to shine with each word.

'I have found transitional integration.'

'I don't understand what that means,' Laura stated.

'No, well, transitional meaning transition and integration meaning unite; I used the power of my mind to go back in time.'

Laura frowned. 'Like meditation.'

'No, I actually transitioned to another time entirely.'

'What?' Laura asked curiously.

'1865. I went back in time,' said the professor.

Laura was disappointed, he was a crank. 'So, you're telling me you went back in time to 1865.'

'Yes,' he beamed.

'How?'

'I visited my relative, who owned a shop in Northcote Road, Battersea, in England. He was my great-great-great grandfather.'

'But — how?'

'I closed my eyes and went through a relaxing process to gain a state of mind I call Concentrated Realisation.'

'I visualised that I was in a whirlpool and kept thinking of the number 1865 and the shop.' He pointed at Laura, 'I have a photo of it, you see.'

'I thought of the shop over and over again, and then, I was actually in 1865 on the steps, before the front door of the tobacco business my ancestor operated.'

'So, you are saying that you met him?' Laura was greatly intrigued but thought this was absurd.

'Yes, I did, and we had tea and chatted. I am not sure he believed me in the beginning, but by the end of my stay, he did. He asked me to return.'

'So, have you been back?'

'Well, now I have fallen down those blasted stairs and I am stuck in this wheelchair, I need someone to go in my place.'

Laura did not realise he was hoping she would be the one to take his place.

'Why do you need someone else to go back? I mean you

have met your ancestor, what more is there?'

'I want to help the hospital but am at my wit's end. The public are not offering the type of funding required.' The professor smiled. 'I have an idea though,' he said almost mischievously.

She decided to humour him, although she thought it all nonsense. There was no such thing as time travel, it just wasn't so.

'I thought if my ancestor bought stamps and kept them hidden somewhere safe for me to find in the future, I could cash them in and the hospital would have its funding. Do you know how valuable stamps are today?'

Laura shook her head.

'Come with me, I'll show you.'

The professor rolled his wheelchair over to a desk and tapped at a laptop. He beckoned for Laura to sit down next to him, so she pulled up a chair. He then brought up a website. There was a little red English stamp with a short description. It was the rarest of all, worth almost a cool 500,000 English pounds. A few of those, and the professor would have millions to spend on his beloved hospital.

Laura was impressed, even though she still thought time travel was a myth.

The professor sensed her skepticism and smiled gently at

her. 'I am asking you to just embark on a trip back into the past, see for yourself.'

'I do not believe in time travel, it won't work. You need to find someone else,' Laura stated rather more sharply than she intended.

'No, you can be a skeptic, that does not matter. Just trust me to send you back into the past.'

Laura sighed.

The first surprise was that the professor asked her to take all her jewellery off and put on a long black coat.

Jeremy was a close friend of the professor, so Laura knew he could be trusted.

As if he read her mind, he said, 'Trust me, and follow my instructions, you will see for yourself.'

'I must tell you a very important thing,' he pondered. 'You cannot take anything of value back with you; it will be lost in the whirlpool of time travel. Also, Laura, an extremely significant point, no one you meet in 1865 can come back with you, they will disintegrate and die.'

Laura frowned, rather surprised at this revelation.

She removed the chain at her throat and handed it to the professor; she had no rings or bracelets. Not even a watch. She then put her handbag to one side, her phone and wallet inside. He urged her to put on a large, black velvet coat, which she did.

'Button it up,' he instructed, 'it will be rather cold there.'

Laura went to take off her shoes before she lay on the sofa.

'No, no, you will need your shoes.'

It dawned on Laura that he actually believed she would be walking down a street in Battersea, England, in 1865. She did not believe any of this but she wanted to help him. It took her mind off other things. She lay down and relaxed.

The professor began to speak to her in a very soothing voice. 'Close your eyes, see yourself at the top of a large, old-fashioned staircase. You can see the steps leading down and you begin to descend.' Laura imagined herself taking the steps.

The professor counted down as she did. 'Ten, nine, eight.' After he mentioned the number one, he said, 'You are now at the bottom of the staircase. You can see a large, open sliding door. You step through it and out into a beautiful garden. It has a swimming pool and a garden seat. There are flower beds brimming with colour. You sit on the seat and go deep within your mind until you feel the integration within your being.

'You also concentrate firstly on the number 1865, seeing it large and bold in your mind, then England, and finally Northcote Road, Battersea. Then you wait. You breathe ever so slowly and you sink deeper into integration.'

After some time, he said, 'You will see a path appear when you are ready.'

After a few moments, Laura said, 'I can see the path.' It was a solid path of flagstones, and each side was overflowing with colourful flowers of every description.

The path had appeared to her right. It continued to grow until at the very end of the garden there was a white picket gate.

'Can you see the gate?' asked the professor.

'Yes.'

'Go on the path now, Laura; keep going until you are at the gate.'

Laura nodded.

The professor noted her feet moved slightly. He was very excited at this.

'Open the gate, Laura.'

She did.

Suddenly, she felt cold. A wind had started up.

The professor noted that her hair was moving as though it had been touched by a breeze, and Laura had begun to fade.

Before her, Laura could see bright, blue lights that seemed to form a circle. This must be the whirlpool of time travel. How could it be possible? There was no such thing! However, she concentrated on 1865. The professor had stressed how important that was. She visualised 1865 in her mind in large figures, then England and finally, Northcote Road, Battersea.

In a faraway voice, the professor said, 'Can you see the tobacco shop?'

Suddenly darkness replaced the circle of light. She saw she was standing on cobblestones and looked ahead. The sign said Johnson's Tobacco & Snuff. Laura was excited.

She could hear the professor's voice, but only faintly. 'Now Laura, I want you to enter the shop and meet Mr Harold Johnson,' said the professor.

Laura was slightly afraid; it felt so real to be here. She could hear horses' hooves and saw people in the distance, dressed in long coats and large hats, walking up the street.

Meanwhile, the professor flinched as Laura disappeared entirely from his sofa.

She pressed against the building and felt somewhat uneasy. Was this really happening?

She opened the door to the shop and immediately could smell tobacco. A distinguished gentleman in his late twenties was sitting behind a mahogany counter and looked up. He had wavy brown hair and wore a long black coat.

'Mr Johnson? Malcolm sent me.'

Chapter 3

HAROLD JOHNSON

After some explanation, Harold Johnson and Laura sat in the tiny, cosy kitchen at the back of the shop. There were no windows, but a comforting fire heated the room. The wooden flooring creaked when you walked on it. Laura's cup was chipped around the edge, but the tea was warm and soothing and she began to feel more at ease.

After she explained the professor's idea about the stamps, Mr Johnson exclaimed, 'I must say this is extraordinary! I have never encountered such a thing in my entire life! For someone to come from another age, the future in fact, and request that I help to assist a hospital I will never see, and more to the point, never benefit from.'

Laura did not know how to respond.

Finally, she said, 'Well, if you don't want to, I'll tell Malcolm.'

'No, no, I didn't mean that!' he said testily. 'I just find the whole thing odd.'

'I know, I do too. I did not believe I could come here at all. I don't believe in time travel.'

Mr Johnson smiled. Laura smiled back.

'Malcolm,' said Mr Johnson, 'what a character he is. I must say, I am rather proud to be related to him.' Laura beamed and sipped her tea. If this could work at all, she thought, it would be a miracle, a nice one.

Later, Mr Johnson gave Laura some soup and a piece of stale bread, which actually was not too bad. She dipped it in the soup, like when she was a little girl, and it warmed her heart. She was apprehensive about leaving. She had to do the ritual correctly in order to get back to the professor.

Mr Johnson brought her to a back room in which there was a wooden bed.

'This is where Malcolm came to "go back" as he put it,' said Mr Johnson. 'Extraordinary.' He smiled at her, and she sat on the bed. He bid her farewell, patting her shoulder. 'I hope to see you again, Laura. Tell Malcolm I will buy the stamps, which should be simple enough, however, finding the right place to hide them, well that is entirely a different matter.'

It was very dark now in the room, with no light and with a faint smell of damp.

Laura went through her ritual, coming back through the circle of light, and then through the white picket gate. Walking up the path, crossing over to the garden and through the double doors, ascending the stairs. With a shock she opened her eyes, only to see the professor smiling expectantly at her.

'Well?' he said.

'I met him, and he agreed to do it.' She sat up.

'Excellent!'

Laura filled him in on all the details and the professor took notes.

'Of course, one of us will have to go back to find out where Mr Johnson will hide the stamps,' she said. It would not be easy, hiding stamps safely so that they may be retrieved more than one hundred and fifty years later!

They went out to dinner, and every time Laura tried to talk about her trip back in time, the professor gently put his hand on her arm. 'Let's just relax for now.' She was excited, but he was cautious.

She wondered if what they were doing was dangerous.

'We need to keep all of this a secret, Laura.'

'Yes of course. I am astonished it happened. I did not believe in it at all.'

'I know,' he laughed, 'I was surprised myself.'

Laura went home to a very quiet house.

She had agreed to visit the professor the following Wednesday. It was crazy, but she was actually looking forward to going back to 1865. Most importantly, she now believed in time travel.

On Wednesday, Laura and the professor sat in the lounge room, drinking tea and eating Madeira cake. Eventually, the two settled excitedly to the task at hand.

Laura returned to Mr Johnson. He too was excited. They sat together, and both were extremely pleased to see each other again.

'Well, I have bought the red stamps, I bought ten of them,' Mr Johnson said.

'That's wonderful!' Laura exclaimed. 'Did you think where to hide them, Mr Johnson?'

'Please, call me Harold,' he smiled.

Laura smiled.

Harold grew sad and said, 'Yes, my beloved sister passed away last month. I thought I could hide them in her grave somehow. The cemetery is very serene, and I believe it will be the safest place for the stamps.'

Laura touched Harold's arm. 'I'm sorry you lost your sister. I lost my husband in an accident recently, so I understand what you are going through.'

'Oh,' said Harold, 'I'm sorry to hear that.'

They sat in silence for a while, then Harold said, 'Well Laura, do you have time for another cup of tea?'

'Yes, I believe I do.'

⁊ℰ

When Laura returned, she talked to the professor, and they came to believe that the stamps would be a feasible solution. The new wing of the hospital would cost nine million, however, they seemed to be short some four million or so. All avenues, both from the government and the public, had been exhausted, and the architect was threatening to pull out. He didn't want to waste his time if funding was not available. The stamps would generate millions in today's money and were the only answer.

The professor and Laura met almost daily. Not to pursue time travel, but merely to chat and drink tea. Going out to lunch became a ritual between the two, who had become great friends.

The following Wednesday, Laura returned to 1865 and Harold Johnson.

They caught a carriage to a small cemetery on the outskirts of Battersea. Laura inspected the grave of Mrs Nancy Johnson Smythe. She was buried with her late husband, Arthur, who had died of diphtheria. Nancy also had succumbed to the disease. The wind grew cold around Laura's shoulders. It seemed such a gloomy day. Harold buried the stamps which were in a small sturdy box. He had brought a trowel for the purpose.

When Laura returned to Parkville and the professor, they sat drinking tea and eating cucumber sandwiches, very pleased that the stamps were now in place.

'Of course, Harold expects you to visit him, as soon as you can walk again,' said Laura, sipping her tea.

'I will,' the professor cleared his throat, 'I have some news, Laura,' he said.

'Next week I am going to Brisbane, to visit my sister there. She says she has made appointments with corporations who may be willing to donate.'

Laura looked sad.

The professor was touched that she would miss him.

'I will only be gone a week. Then we can visit Harold, together. Would you like that?'

'Yes,' said Laura. She had come to rely on him, and now she was afraid that a week without him would be hard.

Chapter 4

THE SINGLE LIFE

Laura found the life insurance policies. The sum insured for Dan was 1.5 million dollars. Reading the policies, it was hard to believe.

The sum insured for her life was two million. The policy on Dan's life was undeniably in place. After making a call to the insurance company, she was assured she would definitely receive the money. Then Laura thought, *well he had my life insured as he was going to organise my death, and now it's he who is dead*. She felt very sad.

Next, she paid bills and sat watching too much TV once again. Her life was empty. There was nothing to do. Most telling of all, there was no Dan, no one to hold and be comforted by. It wasn't long before she came to realise he did not love her when they married, that the plot to end her life was real but he had changed his mind; he had fallen in love with her. This sat easily with her now, and she was able to forgive, although her life seemed to have no purpose.

Diane, her close friend, had been shut out of her life for a while. Now, Laura made the effort to call her and apologise.

'Oh, that's okay. I knew you would get back to me. It must be very hard without Daniel.'

There was silence for a while then Diane said, 'Hey, I'm going to the Stanton Club on Saturday; wanna come? I mean, you don't have to meet anyone, just to get together, you know?'

Why not, thought Laura. It probably would do her good.

They met at Diane's apartment in South Yarra. It was a very white apartment, with modern art everywhere. It seemed a bit lifeless to Laura.

Diane had jet-black hair and a pretty face. She had cut her hair short, and it suited her perfectly. She wore a revealing, long blue dress, with lots of silver jewellery and a fake Cartier watch.

Laura had dressed in a long, dark green dress, that had beading at the neck and long sleeves. She wore low-heeled, black patent shoes and carried a small, silver handbag. She wore no jewellery. Her brown hair was pinned up with a black metal hair grip.

They entered the Stanton Club to loud, pulsating music, and Diane shouted, 'Let's sit at a private table!'

Laura nodded and followed her.

The Stanton had chairs and roomy, circular sofas, decked out in purple and silver. The far wall was brick with multi-coloured lights.

It did not look like a club; more like a subdued restaurant. It was very popular, although not a crazy place to dance in, more a place for adults who wanted to meet new people and enjoy an evening out.

Diane came back to the table with two drinks, gin and tonic for herself, a Diet Coke for Laura.

'You wanna get some tasters?' Laura who was feeling peckish, nodded.

'Hold on.' Diane rushed off once more to the bar, and then came back with a plate of treats. A trio of dips with toasted Turkish bread, a dozen crispy chicken pieces, as well as potato wedges with tomato dipping sauce.

Eventually, Diane got up to dance with a friendly-looking guy. She smiled back at Laura.

A tall, dark handsome man slid onto the sofa, close to Laura. 'Hi, I'm Joe, how are you?'

Laura nodded. She was a bit surprised.

'Can I be your friend?' Joe said as he leaned into her. Laura realised he was drunk. Since divorcing herself from alcohol, she had no desire to deal with drunks. She moved away from him.

'Wonder if you would like to go out with me sometime.' He said it as a statement, not a question.

Laura smiled. 'I just came here for the music.'

He frowned, then nodded and left. She sighed, noticing that Diane had gone to the bar and was sitting with her dance partner. They were happily chatting.

Later, Laura went to the bar and got another Diet Coke. She did not make eye contact with Diane; she didn't wish to interrupt anything that may have been promising. Diane was never happy with her current partner; they would only last a few months and she would want someone new.

When Laura came back to the table, she sat drinking her Coke and enjoying the music. It was not music she knew, but it was great.

A man approached her. 'Mind if I sit down?'

Laura smiled.

His name was Vincent, and he was a real estate agent. He was tall, had blue eyes, and had cut his brown hair very short, so that only a few inches of hair on top remained. They chatted about Melbourne weather; he told her all about his career. Laura politely listened although he didn't come up for air. Then he said, 'You want to go somewhere else with me?'

'Where?' she said.

Vincent cleared his throat. 'There's a motel with a great

coffee shop around the corner.'

Laura frowned.

He was not wearing a wedding ring but the imprint of one was evident.

Laura suddenly didn't want to be there. 'Only one problem,' she said.

'What's that?'

'I'm allergic to married men.'

He looked startled.

Laura stood up and collected her handbag.

'Excuse me,' she said and smiled sweetly. Maybe this club was just a pickup joint.

She headed for the door.

Laura waved at Diane, who stood up and came towards her.

'Think I'll push off if you don't mind, I'm going to get Lionel to pick me up.' Lionel was Laura's regular Uber driver.

'Fair enough,' Diane giggled. She seemed tipsy, and if Laura was to be truthful, she needed to get away from people who embraced alcohol. In fact, it could be dangerous for her; although she was sure she would never pick up another drink, it was always a far-off possibility. A dangerous one.

'Will you call me tomorrow?' said Diane.

'Yes,' said Laura and left the club.

Sheltering from the soft rain, she called Lionel.

Once she entered her home, the door closed gently behind her, and the gloom descended like a black cloud. She felt tears sting her eyes.

She collapsed on the bed in the dark, not even removing her shoes, and reached for the lamp. She saw Dan's aftershave on the bedside table. His pocket watch, which he never had worn, and a small silver box with his signet ring inside. She was not ready to pack up his belongings and give them to charity. She missed him; his possessions were all she had now. She also missed the professor.

A thought came to her, and though she knew she shouldn't, she closed her eyes and went into deep transitional integration. She embraced 'concentrated realisation' and her mood lifted; she was suddenly filled with excitement. She wouldn't stay long; she would just visit Harold Johnson and have a chat. Well, that was the plan.

In her dreamy state of transition, she saw the year as 1765, not realising her mistake. Next, she focused on England and finally … what was the address again? As she was trying to recall it, she visualised herself descending the stairs as usual and sitting on the outside garden seat. Then she saw the path and the white picket gate. Becoming very excited, Laura hurried along the path and opened the gate.

She felt a cool breeze on her face, then the bright, blue light forming the circle she knew well. She was entering the whirlpool. Laura then felt strange and opened her eyes. She had transitioned. However, she was in an open area with trees. She didn't recognise anything. There was certainly no tobacco shop. Well, she thought, I will just keep going, it will probably sort itself out. She had a nagging thought, *could she be in the wrong place*? Harold Johnson could be just a short distance away but then again ... maybe not.

She took a path with crushed pebbles and felt rain upon her face. She could hear her footsteps echoing back at her.

There was a sudden sound coming from behind, but she didn't have time to turn around, something struck her back with great force, and she fell forward, hitting her head on the stone border of the path. The darkness engulfed her, and she lay unconscious with the soft rain still falling on her face.

Sir James Harrington dismounted his horse, Captain, and rushed to the young woman who lay before him.

'Oh my God!' he exclaimed, pushing a strand of blond hair back, and kneeling down beside her.

'Are you alright?'

There was no response, and James realised he may have done this person great harm. His horse was a lively, jet-black stallion and had knocked the young lady off her feet. He lifted her limp body onto Captain and gently rode home to Harrington Manor.

The mansion stood on many acres of land, an imposing brown brick structure. He called for Henry, his manservant, who hurriedly came to help.

'Take her,' said James urgently, 'put her on my bed, and send Jacob to get Dr Stevenson, he must come, it's very urgent!'

'Yes sir,' said Henry and carried Laura into the house. He was a middle-aged man, tall with black hair and a rather weather-beaten face.

With Laura in the bedroom, Mrs Jones the housekeeper brought a jug of water and a glass. She also covered Laura with a blanket and sat nearby waiting patiently for the doctor.

Later that day, Dr Stevenson came out of the bedroom and touched James on the arm.

'No real harm, old chap, I think it best you leave her be. She will probably wake up of her own accord in a few hours or maybe longer, maybe tomorrow. There is no real damage.'

James looked uncertain.

'Don't look so worried; she should rest for a few days, then you can take her home. By the way, who is she, where is she from?'

'I have no idea. But you say she will be alright, she will recover?'

'She will be fine.' Dr Stevenson, a rotund man with bright red hair, walked with James to the front door. He peered at James. 'Do not worry.' The doctor smiled.

They parted, with James thanking the doctor for coming at such short notice.

He put his hand on the door of the bedroom and pushed it open, only to see the young lady with her eyes closed.

'She is going to be alright, don't you worry,' said Mrs Jones assuredly.

'Yes, so I believe. I thought I may have— well, you know.'

'She's going to wake up tonight or tomorrow.' Mrs Jones's face crinkled up in a smile and her many wrinkles became more predominant. Her grey curls framed a kindly face underneath a white bonnet. She wore a brown dress with white lace at the neck and a cream-coloured lace shawl around her shoulders, tied at the front. She had worked for the Harrington family for many years, moving in there after her beloved husband had died. It was as though the Manor had become the main thing in her life. She thought Sir James was kind and thoughtful; he never lost his temper with human or beast. It was just a great pity he was a very sad individual.

'I'd love a cup of tea, Margaret, if you don't mind.'

'Yes sir.' And with that, Mrs Jones left the room.

James tentatively moved towards the bed. She was a

beautiful young woman in a dark green dress lying on his bed with a blanket draped over her. She had a peaceful look, but he was very concerned.

The bedroom had large glass-paned doors that led out to the gardens of Harrington Manor. James opened them. The smell of roses came to him, and the peacocks on the property called to each other in the dying light of the afternoon.

James sat by the doors at a little table with high-backed chairs. Mrs Jones brought his tea accompanied by some freshly baked biscuits.

She eyed him with concern. 'I've readied the Rosemary Room for you to sleep in tonight, sir.' She stood erect with her hands clasped in front of her.

'Thank you, Mrs Jones, you're too kind.'

'Not at all, is there anything else you need?'

James looked sad and glanced up at her. 'No,' he simply said.

Chapter 5

SIR JAMES HARRINGTON

Sir James Harrington was very alone in the world. Most of his relatives had passed away. He missed his parents but had grown to accept his life without them. What was hard to accept was the way the world was. The inequality in London. It bothered him that the poor were dying, sometimes in poor-houses like prisons, with meagre food and water. They would simply waste away. The babies who died at just a few days old filled him with such sadness, there had been times he felt extreme emotional pain and would spend hours up on the Lincolnshire cliffs, contemplating ending it all. However, if he did, he would not be forgiven by God. James was a dedicated Christian, or so he thought. But for the last few years he had felt anger towards a God who allowed such suffering.

He was a tall man, strong and handsome. He always wore his blond hair tied back with a black ribbon and had the bluest of eyes. Sometimes people were taken aback at his eyes. James was an intense individual, twenty-eight years old and single. There were rumours about his unusual behaviour, his tendency to be emotional, sad. To some, he was a mystery. People did not understand how he could be sad; James Harrington was very rich. Harrington Manor boasted nine hundred acres of pure, rich land, with a mansion to suit. He could not have been more advantaged and yet he seemed extremely unhappy with life. He did indulge in possessions to some extent; he was known for always being immaculately dressed and was thought of by those that did not know him well, as unusual. He never corrected their miscalculated opinion of him, seeming not to care. At times he annoyed the aristocrats and royals with his aloofness, paying them no mind, preferring to be without company. Then surprisingly he would invite them all to the Manor for an evening party, which would be very well organised and most enjoyable.

James also had a habit of bathing. Doctors thought frequent bathing was bizarre behaviour and rather unhealthy at that. Many of the servants at the Manor saw Jacob, Henry's young understudy, gathering water, heating it and bringing it to James's bathroom, only to carry it off afterwards. It was a tedious ritual that James insisted upon every single day.

He also owned many colognes. He was constant in these behaviours, and yet people thought it served no purpose.

One dreadful day in the middle of winter, James was on the cliffs when it had grown dark. He put a pistol to his head, closed his eyes and pulled the trigger. But it malfunctioned and just then, lightning filled the sky. He looked to the skies, fearful. He took this as a sign from God that he was not meant to die and so he resigned himself to living.

The next evening he sat in the chapel at Harrington Manor. He felt the gloom of the place, despite the soft light of the many candelabras. The pungent fragrance of flowers filled the air and he could smell the oak wood of the pew as he knelt before the altar, his hands clasped together. He felt drained, sad. There was a misery inching to overtake him.

Why was he so melancholy, why could he not fight to become more stable? He felt on edge most days, sinking further into the dread of this miserable life.

He had walked without energy from the chapel to the gardens. The night was crisp, and he heard the faint call of a fox in the darkness. His breath filled the cold air with gentle, white puffs. The wet grass beneath him offered its fresh, clean scent, having been mown that morning.

His mind raced: he needed to be grateful for the fortunate life he had, and yet others stirred his heart, for they had nothing. He wanted so much to help, but it was difficult to manifest endurance, and really, was there any point? He oscillated between wanting to help and feeling helpless to do so.

James had great friends; he was fond of his cousin Nicholas, who was Lord Lawrence. His best friend was Nigel Matthews, the Earl of Berrisfordshire and, Sir Hugh Williams who if truth be told was tolerated these days by James rather than embraced in friendship. Hugh was prone to drinking, gambling and fornication, all to excess. He owned and ran Willow Farm, which just happened to be a huge success.

They all had urged James to marry, but he saw marriage as a sacred thing and the marriages he was privy to were anything but. Many marriages were arranged and had nothing to do with love. Also, mistresses were a fact of life.

Often married couples felt contempt for each other. This was common with marriages arranged for financial gain, so much so that the couple would live separate lives. He did not wish that for himself, and so he remained single.

Chapter 6

MARY ELIZABETH

James owned a staggering amount of land, which ended at Berriman Road. A young heiress, Mary Elizabeth Witton, owned the land beyond, with an imposing mansion. She also had more servants than James.

A marriage between the two would ensure a prosperous future.

Nigel had arranged for James to meet the lady. There was an afternoon tea at Harrington Manor. Several acquaintances attended and when Mary Elizabeth arrived, Nigel introduced her to James.

She was a little stout and had an unappealing face framed by dark hair; however, James pressed on. She was an aristocrat and definitely a possibility. Nigel had compelled him to meet her, so he felt obliged to do so. What harm could it do? He may end up married, which would be a good thing.

All the guests at the afternoon tea knew exactly why

they were there. Some grinned knowingly. Others seemed concerned for their sad friend. Was he finally going to marry and be happy?

The meeting with Mary Elizabeth was proceeding well, if one could describe it as that, until she struck her maid with a riding whip. It was one decent crack on the maid's shoulder. She had brought the wrong umbrella. Mary Elizabeth also chastised Henry for the way he performed his duties, and finally turned her sights on James.

'I don't like the colour of your home's interior.' Her tight black curls moving back and forth, her forehead creased.

James said nothing.

'As Lady Harrington, I would have to make changes.' James, standing by the fireplace, simply bowed. She continued, 'The furniture is not to my taste.' She gestured to the offending pieces.

'Just how many acres do you have?' she said, straightening her back and looking at him with what could only be described as suspicion.

Again, James did not answer, he was in shock.

'I am not about to enter into anything that does not come up to my standard, I am not going to bow down to any man at all!'

'Neither should you,' James said quietly. And then it struck him, he could not possibly live with this woman. He could barely stand to speak to her.

'However,' she continued, 'marriage between us would be favourable to our joint prosperity.' It was then and only then, crossing the room, she smiled up at him.

James bowed again.

'By the way, what sort of investments do you dabble in, you need to watch your money, you know.' She pointed to him dramatically, the smile fading.

Her voice was loud and the other guests looked away, embarrassed for James. At the end of the afternoon tea, everyone was a little subdued at Mary Elizabeth's words; they certainly were not used to a forceful woman speaking her mind. When the last of the guests had left, James and Nigel went for a walk in the gardens.

'So,' started Nigel, 'do you think you will marry Mary Elizabeth?'

'I do not wish to marry her, and I certainly do not wish to bed her. That woman does not inspire romance in the slightest!' He gestured with his hand.

Then James caught Nigel's eye.

'You seem disappointed.'

Nigel sighed, 'I just thought with her fortune and yours, any offspring would be well provided for.'

James turned and looked at his friend, who had stopped walking.

'Thank you for your concern for my offspring. Come, I feel like riding. Do you fancy a race?'

Nigel smiled and nodded. 'Do you wish to have a wager?'

James was smiling. He had completely put the disastrous afternoon behind him.

Nigel, however, was determined to find a lady for his friend. It was very important. James was twenty-eight years old now; time he married.

Chapter 7

GENEVIEVE MASTERSON

A month later, another afternoon tea took place at Harrington Manor. A young lady named Genevieve Masterson was eighteen years old and quite pretty. She had a pale face and black hair and was petite. She also had a missing tooth, not that it was terribly noticeable. This, James thought, was not something to hold against her, indeed she appeared to be a suitable contender for his consideration.

She also came from a family who were well connected financially as well as socially.

James was cordial and seemed happy to chat with his guests, as well as Genevieve.

However, there came a time when the young lady displayed a habit which was rather hard to ignore. She giggled in a manner that was rather unpleasant.

She may have been nervous; however, as the afternoon

progressed, she giggled more, and James knew she was not the one. Rather too young for him, he thought, rather unintelligent if he wished to be unkind, and that giggle was, well, not something he could possibly live with.

Nigel meant well, but it was all in vain.

At the end of the day, James felt dejected and defeated. Finding a wife was no easy task.

'James,' said Nigel, 'you can find romance on the side; at least marry someone who fits your wealth, your position.' He motioned with his hands in the air. Then you can take as many mistresses as your heart desires, love is a short-lived thing anyway, my dear chap.'

But James looked doubtful.

'I disapprove of your view of love, Nigel; I do not wish to live like that. Rather, I would live alone than marry and it be a lie.' He looked intensely at Nigel, who raised his eyebrows.

'You are a long-suffering fellow; I am glad I do not see life as you. Come along, let's ride, I have a match for Captain,' he said smiling. 'I bought a stallion at High Meadow stables yesterday.'

Nigel decided to let James find his own lady.

Chapter 8

THE MEETING

The morning was misty, and James woke early. After his bath, he shaved, dressed, then went to Mrs Jones in the kitchen. She was surprised to see him so early.

'Is the young lady alright?' He did not himself feel alright, he had hardly slept.

'Yes, I looked in on her first thing, she has not stirred. I will sit with her shortly, when I finish preparing breakfast.'

'I'll sit with her,' he said, 'I am anxious to be there and apologise for myself and Captain. What a terrible thing to happen.' James pushed a wayward strand of blond hair back.

'It wasn't your fault, sir; I am sure the young lady will be alright.'

'I hope so.'

'Here, your tea, sir.' Mrs Jones handed him a cup and saucer. 'Would you like some breakfast?'

'No, not now, I'll bring my tea to the bedroom.'

'Very good, sir,' she said.

Mrs Jones smiled; suddenly a thought came to her. Maybe he felt something for the young lady; he had no wife, he was such a troubled soul.

James opened the door to the bedroom slowly. The large, glass-paned doors were open, and a light breeze rattled them.

He entered quietly, closing them, sat down at the small table with the high-backed chairs, and sipped his tea.

He looked over tentatively at the young lady who lay motionless in his bed. He felt a surge of guilt at what had happened.

He stayed, hopeful that she would wake up. But she never did. It came time for him to go to Nigel's; they had decided to talk business that morning.

Mrs Jones came to sit with the young woman as soon as she was able.

When Laura opened her eyes, she was unsure where she was. It was a spacious, light room, and the bed she lay in was enormous. She remembered that she had been walking down a path and suddenly she had been pushed, and she had fallen. She remembered nothing beyond that.

An elderly lady sat embroidering on the far side of the room. Suddenly she looked up and smiled.

'There you are.' She stood up.

'Now don't worry, you had a little accident. You've been seen to by the doctor, and he said you would wake up and be alright.'

Laura had the strange feeling that something was not right. She also had a headache. She asked, 'Who are you?'

'I'm Mrs Jones, I work for Sir James. This is his home, and he told me to look after you.'

'Sir James?'

'Yes, of Harrington Manor, he is the master my lady.'

When Mrs Jones called her my lady, Laura thought *this must be 1865. I am just in the wrong part of England, that's all.*

She tried to sit up. Mrs Jones rushed to straighten her pillows and smiled at her.

'Can I ask you something?' said Laura.

'Yes?'

'What year is it?'

'Why, 1765,' said Mrs Jones, puzzled at the question.

Laura was startled, 'And where is Harrington Manor exactly?'

'Lincolnshire, my lady.'

Laura was shocked. Not only did she have the wrong address, she had the wrong century! She tried to be calm, *it will be alright.* She would simply go back, she had done it before, and she could do it again.

'What is your name if you don't mind me askin', my lady?'

'Laura Wesley.'

'I'm Margaret Jones. And where are you from?'

Laura did not know what to say.

'You wouldn't know it; it's not well known.' She smiled. 'I need the bathroom.'

Mrs Jones attempted to help Laura out of bed but was assured she was fine.

Once in the bathroom, it was not what Laura had expected. The toilet was strange, there was no running water and a large porcelain bath stood in the middle of the room.

'Do you think I could take a bath?'

Laura looked down at herself. She was dressed in the white nightgown Mrs Jones had managed to put on her. She touched the fabric. 'Does this belong to Sir James's wife or is it yours?'

Mrs Jones was amused. 'No, it belongs to the Countess of Berrisfordshire. She is such a nice lady; I am sure she will not mind.'

'Who is the Countess?'

'Sir James is good friends with the Earl of Berrisfordshire. He and his wife stay at the Manor on occasion.'

Mrs Jones had carefully washed Laura's green dress, as well

as her strange underwear, and decided it was best to try and get some clothing for her. What Laura had arrived in seemed inappropriate attire. With that in mind, she had ventured into the Oak Room. As his best friend, Nigel Matthews, with his wife Jennifer, the Countess of Berrisfordshire, often stayed at Harrington Manor, and enjoyed the Oak Room as a permanent guest room. Mrs Jones returned from there with four dresses, undergarments, stockings and even a pair of shoes as she thought the low-heeled, black patent shoes that Laura arrived in unusual. Also in the collection were feathers, pearls, white powder and rouge. Laura was sitting in the bathroom when Mrs Jones put all the clothing on the bed. She carefully placed everything else on a large cabinet by the windows.

'I will get water organised for your bath.'

Laura looked at the toilet. 'I am not sure about this.'

Mrs Jones was puzzled.

'Where does it all go?'

'All go, my lady?'

'Yes, the business.'

'Jacob takes everything away at the end of the day. You can use it.'

Laura grimaced.

Mrs Jones left, and Laura went to the toilet then poured

water from a jug into a bowl and washed her hands. She looked at herself in the huge mirror. There was a small chest of drawers with unlit candles and holders, little dishes with soap, and towels piled on another cabinet.

In the middle of the afternoon, when Laura had finished her bath, she chose to wear a floral-patterned dress which fitted well enough. She managed to pin her hair up but did not touch any of the other things.

She looked fine or so she thought until Mrs Jones tried to persuade her to put some feathers in her hair and to dab some rouge on her cheeks and lips. Laura declined.

'I'm fine, really,' Laura said.

At that time there was a knock on the door, and Mrs Jones answered. Henry explained that Sir James had returned.

She whispered to Henry that the lady's name was Laura Wesley and that she was awake, had dressed and would no doubt require something to eat.

Henry found Sir James in the Rosemary Room. He was dressed mainly in cream-coloured apparel, his jacket sporting silver buttons. Underneath was a burgundy waistcoat, and he wore black boots. His hair was tied back, as usual, with a black ribbon.

'Henry,' he said.

Henry explained that the young lady was named Laura

Wesley and that Mrs Jones was going to give her a meal shortly.

'Ah, I shall join her, introduce myself, what?'

'Very good, sir,' Henry bowed and left.

James ventured down to the kitchen; the staff were surprised at this. He ordered the kitchen staff to prepare a good meal, to be served in the Green Room, which was reserved for special guests. The workers were all a-twitter with excitement, mainly because they had never seen Sir James so spirited.

He then went to enter the west wing but remembered that the young lady had his bedroom, so he went to the guest quarters, the Rosemary Room, and viewed himself in the mirror. He put some cologne on. Mrs Jones and Henry had transported his things earlier. He was excited at meeting Laura officially, and he thought to himself, *thank goodness she is alright.*

He went and sat in the Green Room. The staff fussed around him arranging flowers, dishes, trays of food and glasses. The main butler, Gerald, stood stoic at the door.

Henry stood close to James.

When Mrs Jones came into the room, James stood up and smiled cordially as he saw Laura. She wore a white dress with a floral pattern. Her beautiful chestnut hair was piled up and she had large brown eyes. As she came close, he offered her a chair before Henry could do the same.

'I'm James Harrington, Baronet, at your service.'

'Laura,' she simply said and was startled as James took her hand and kissed it.

She remembered that this practice was common in this period.

Laura sat down and tried to arrange her dress. It was beautiful, but she was not used to it. It had deep pockets and a length of material at the back, which trailed along the floor. *Extremely impractical*, she thought.

James explained about the accident and how the doctor had been summoned immediately.

He served her chicken and vegetable soup. At the end of two more courses of fish, then meat and vegetables, they finished with fruit and custard. James accidentally touched her hand. *Laura is beautiful,* he thought, *and she has lovely teeth.* He suddenly thought of Genevieve's smile.

Laura smiled at him, and he felt a strangeness in his stomach. He looked at her intently, thinking the last time he felt like this around a woman was back in Paris with Franchette.

James had been in France years prior for business, when a country girl named Franchette La Blanc began to pursue him. He had known he was not in love with her, but she was a willing participant in their lovemaking. They had gone for long walks, and her cooking was quite delightful. She was petite, had a chubby face and bright blue eyes. Her hair was brown, very curly and he loved how she was not particularly reserved like the English. She laughed at his French.

He was fluent in the language, or so he thought, until she would giggle at some of his pronunciations. His mother, Lady Emily Harrington, had spoken French, and he had delighted in learning the language.

He failed to be a chaste, religious man with Franchette and felt guilty about it; however, at the same time, she was sweet, made no demands on him and lightened his mood considerably. James had asked her if she was afraid of him when they were in bed. He always wanted to be a gentleman, but the act of love could be ... well, something else entirely when in the throes of passionate lovemaking. She had answered no, but he thought she was, and also, she was too docile for his taste. She seemed to allow the act of love to happen, without really participating.

Eventually, James's business interests demanded his attention, so he returned to England. He always meant to send for her, to invent some reason she could stay at Harrington Manor. But as his sadness progressed about the state of the world, the poor people in it, and how unfair life was, he sank into a fog which he did not have the energy to fight. He was always riding, spending long days at the coast, sitting on the beach until he froze.

He had watched the poor people, struggling to survive, sink deeper into resentment. Fighting to stay alive while many were starving to death in the bowels of London.

He didn't want to care, but he did, very deeply, as though God had deemed him his servant in solving this problem. But the more time and effort he invested, the more insurmountable it seemed.

The poor suffered from many ailments, not just disease. There was the unfairness brought upon them by the aristocrats, and after all, James was an aristocrat, he could not deny it.

But even more horrible were the likes of Mary Elizabeth who constantly tormented servants and footmen; she showed great disdain for the poor and would wield her power wherever she went. He saw her for what she really was, a tyrant. He had not realised how evil the woman was and shuddered when he thought of the time he had considered marrying her.

James poured some cognac into a glass, but Laura said, 'I don't drink alcohol, I'd rather a cup of tea, if you don't mind.'

It was then he ascertained that she was refined, but he could not place the accent.

James signalled to Henry, who motioned to Gerald, and Laura was served with tea.

They had eyed each other and smiled, but very little was said until James thought he should offer his well-thought-out apology.

However, just then Laura said, 'I know you cannot possibly believe what I am about to tell you. You may not even know about time travel, but it is what I am involved in.'

James looked up. 'Time travel.'

'Yes, I came here by mistake from another time,' Laura saw he was puzzled, 'in your future,' she added.

'Right,' said James, unsure of what was developing.

Laura explained everything to him about her skepticism, the professor, her visit to 1865, and how she had not focused on that year when she came through the whirlpool and had in error come to be on the path where he encountered her. She also explained that she actually lived in the twenty-first century and that she came from Australia, which was not to be claimed until Captain James Cook acquired it for the English king in 1778.

'Is it a colony?'

She nodded.

'Well, how extraordinary!'

'I know you cannot believe a word I am saying, however, the important thing is I have to go back, and then you can forget all about this bizarre incident.'

James held up his hand and smiled. 'I do know of time travel,' he said, slightly amused, 'come with me.'

They went into the library where James walked over to a large bookcase that dominated the room.

'You have a lot of books!' Laura exclaimed, looking up at the shelves that seemed to go on forever.

James pulled out a book and opened it.

'There,' he said, 'I read this some years ago. I do know what you are talking about.' He handed her the book.

He was standing close to her and loved her eyes; they had such expression when she spoke.

'This particular book was actually banned,' he said, smiling.

She turned and sat down to read.

After some time, she closed the book gently. 'I need to get back,' she said and then explained how she would go into transitional integration.

James said, 'But you have to stay for a few days, the doctor said you should rest.'

Laura thought about the comment, then said, 'I could stay

awhile, I suppose. I feel a bit tired.'

'Well then, you need to recover; the Manor is at your disposal. Anything you need or want, I shall provide. I feel I need to make amends after what happened.' James bowed his head.

'It was an accident, I don't hold you responsible in any way, Sir James.'

The mere mention of his name from her lips made his heart quicken.

He suddenly felt excited and said, 'I would like to show you the Rose Garden, it has some truly lovely specimens this time of year.'

Laura looked thrilled and said, 'I would like that.'

They ventured outside, the sun was high in the sky and there was bird song. James stood close to Laura and offered his arm. Laura took it; she thought it a very quaint gesture. They strode into the Rose Garden, and James named some of the roses. 'My mother, Lady Emily Harrington, created all of this.'

Laura nodded. 'Is your mother here, or does she live elsewhere?'

'Both my parents have passed away.'

'Oh, I am sorry; I understand only too well, my husband has also passed away.'

James was slightly surprised. He had never thought of her as married.

'I offer you my sympathies. Was he very young?'

'He was twenty-eight, there was an accident.' Laura did not elaborate; James would never understand the concept of cars.

James straightened; he was twenty-eight also. Although it was a sad thing, he also felt positive that there could very well be a chance at love here. He had not felt this way in a very long time.

Laura continued, 'I received a large sum of money when he died, but I was at a loose end until I met the professor.' She sounded enthusiastic.

'The professor, is he young?'

'No, rather elderly, but such a vibrant person, I enjoy his company. He is my friend.'

Laura walked over to a large rose bush. 'This is quite lovely,' she said, fingering it.

'That is the Tudor rose, very popular I believe,' said James. *She probably knows nothing of the Wars of the Roses,* he thought.

James felt awkward; she was looking at him intensely. 'Well, Madam,' he said, 'time for another cup of tea I think.' He again held out his arm and she took it. The English drink a lot of tea she remembered.

'Sir James, I just wanted to let you know Mrs Jones refers to me as my lady. I am not titled.'

James smiled. 'Well, I think she is just being respectful. If you wish me to say something to her, I—'

Laura shook her head, 'Oh no, it's fine, she's lovely, very kind.'

Definitely modest, he thought. *Beautiful, considerate, enchanting, stirs a man's heart.*

'By the way, Sir James, do you mind not calling me Madam, I don't particularly like it.' Laura looked up at him.

'Only if you stop calling me sir. James will suffice.' They both grinned.

James bowed. Laura found it alluring. Then when he had kissed her hand, she had felt excited. She was sure he was not aware.

'Oh, I almost forgot, I have a present for you, my dear.' James smiled.

Laura raised her eyebrows, surprised. He then presented her with a locket.

'Oh, James, it's beautiful.' It was oval shaped with diamonds and rubies embedded in gold and hung from a gold chain. She realised he gifted the locket to her to make amends for the accident, but felt it was way too valuable.

'I hope you enjoy it.'

'You know I cannot take it back with me. The professor was very specific about that.'

James looked puzzled.

'Well,' said Laura 'the professor told me that I cannot take things from my era with me when I time travel to the past, and I cannot bring anything along when I return. Also, no person can come back with me, they would simply disintegrate and die.' She smiled but nodded her head solemnly.

James was stunned.

'Well I never,' he said, then smiled mischievously, 'so don't go back.'

Laura raised her hand and laughed. He was flirting with her, and the astonishing thing was that she was receptive.

※

Laura had become overwhelmed and excited that she was actually in this era, in this mansion, experiencing things that were amazing! She grew acquainted with the Manor; it had very high ceilings and huge tapestries hung from the walls as did magnificent paintings in gold frames. Candelabras were everywhere. Giant vases with fresh flowers seemed to greet you at every turn, and the furniture was quite solid. Servants were always around, cleaning, dusting, polishing. *What a life,* she thought.

One particularly large portrait hanging in the main drawing room was of a handsome man, exceptionally attired. Laura thought it must be a Harrington relative, however Gerald told her it was of the current King of England, George III, who just happened to be a dear friend of Sir James.

She knew that in 1765 aristocrats and the royals would have ruled everything, owned everything and were probably very self-centred. At least, this was her opinion. She was never one to pay attention to history classes at school, however, she was of the view that the poor of this era were hard done by. The world now was a very different place, in some ways better but in some ways worse. Hopefully it was more humanitarian than James's world here and now.

Laura was sitting by the fireplace in the main drawing room when James came to her and sat down smiling.

'You look very happy,' she said.

'I am, indeed, I am. I have just received word that my good friends Nigel and Jennifer are returning from Paris on Wednesday. I can't wait to see them.'

The next few days were spent happily enough. James showed her the maze, which she fell in love with and tried to get to the other side of, though always unsuccessfully. When she retreated back to the start, upon seeing her, he would laugh and she would too.

He would sometimes go out on business but returned always in time for afternoon tea with Laura. It became a time for pleasant conversation, and he enjoyed her delightful company.

Laura felt slightly uneasy knowing that Nigel and Jennifer would arrive at the Manor soon. James was an aristocrat, as was the earl and his wife, the countess. Was she supposed to call Nigel 'your lordship', or something equally superficial? Were these people even aware of the suffering that must be happening to the poor in London? She did not know how she knew; it must be something she was taught at school, long ago. The aristocrats, she felt, were purely interested in having a good time and they did not care that the poor were in dire straits. Laura grew a little resentful on their behalf.

When she looked around at the opulence of James's home, his mansion, it occurred to her that he was obscenely rich and she disapproved, vigorously.

Staff at the Manor noticed that James had not gone for a ride to the coast since Laura had appeared. He was a kind employer; everyone liked him and wanted the best for him. They knew he was sad at times, and he often sank further into the depths of despair.

Now, however, he was spending time with Laura, and she had definitely lifted his mood.

One evening James stepped out into the gardens. He felt the thrum of rain, heavy and refreshing. The scent awakened one's senses like a slap. He breathed in, delighted, and felt happy. Yes, happy. He hadn't thought of, nor felt it, in a very long time. He knew why and smiled. Laura.

Chapter 9

THE EARL VISITS

On Wednesday morning there was a lot of rushing around by staff. Mrs Jones was so busy cooking she had not come to see Laura. At 11:45 that morning, a shiny black carriage pulled up outside Harrington Manor and a beautiful fair-haired woman was assisted out of the carriage by Henry, followed by her husband, Nigel Matthews. He had blond hair and a prominent nose. They both were ushered into the vast hallway where James was waiting.

'My dear Jennifer, how I have missed you.' James then kissed her extended hand.

Jennifer was dressed in a wide, light-cream dress. She wore a pink hat with feathers and ribbons, and she also wore white gloves.

'I say, Nigel, you are looking well. Paris must have agreed with you, what?'

Nigel was dressed in a very pale, green jacket, white shirt, breeches and stockings. He wore a lot of lace at the neck as well as black shoes. He smiled warmly at his dear friend.

Jennifer spoke to James about Paris, enquiring about how things were at the Manor, and learning about Laura.

As the guests were ushered into the Green Room, James tugged at the bellpull wherein Henry appeared.

'Can you let Mrs Wesley know we are about to start lunch?'

'Yes, sir,' said Henry.

Jennifer narrowed her eyes. 'Is she—'

'Widowed,' said James, cutting her off.

Jennifer grinned.

Laura was dressed in a pale-blue gown and felt rather conscious that it belonged to Jennifer. She only had Mrs Jones's word that the countess would not mind.

When Laura entered the room, James stood up and said, 'Nigel, Jennifer, this is Laura Wesley, my guest.'

Jennifer rushed over to Laura.

'I hope you don't mind; I've borrowed some of your things,' said Laura awkwardly.

Jennifer was very excited. She took hold of Laura's hands and said, 'I am so thrilled to meet you, I cannot believe it.' She glanced at James. 'So, when are you two going to marry?'

James and Laura were frozen in stunned silence.

James eventually said, 'You say the darnedest things, Jennifer, without really thinking.' He then laughed, trying to give credence to his statement, although he felt extremely awkward.

'Oh well, this one,' Jennifer said, grabbing at James's arm, 'is a very good man. I wanted him to be married years ago, however sadness has prevailed in his life, and it was not to be.' She pouted.

James looked embarrassed. Jennifer then said, 'You know me, James, I always speak my mind.'

'Absolutely know that,' he smiled, relaxing a bit.

'Would you like to have some lunch?' he said, changing the subject entirely.

At that moment, the Earl came across and held Laura's hand, kissing it. He had very blue eyes and a kindly face. His blond hair was tied back with a black ribbon, in much the same way James wore his hair.

'Nigel Matthews, at your service. I am delighted to make your acquaintance. By the way, where are you from?'

James cut Nigel off by saying, 'Come along, let's eat, I'm hungry.'

Laura smiled, relieved.

They all sat down and were served an amazing lunch. One the staff, including Mrs Jones, had slaved over.

The conversation was of trivial things: clothing, shoes, and parties in Paris attended by the Matthews, as well as many things seen and purchased.

At the end of the day they left, and Jennifer turned and waved to Laura who was standing at the front door. She waved back and smiled. They were pleasant but so pretentious her head spun.

When James and Laura were sitting in the large sitting room, he turned to her and said, 'Well, how do you like my friends?'

'Well, you are an aristocrat, as are the Earl and Countess. Do you ever think of the less fortunate in your insignificant lives?'

James looked perplexed, unsure what to say.

'How many pairs of shoes do you have?'

'I don't know — um, thirty-seven or thereabouts.' He frowned at the question. James was known to dress exceptionally well and did not resent the cost of keeping his wardrobe up to a high standard. Even his good friend King George had commented on how marvellously James dressed for social occasions.

'Do you ever think that the poor might benefit from having just one pair of those shoes?'

'Say what?' James's words were hardly audible; he was shocked.

'That is the point I am trying to make! You only care about yourself! You probably are totally unaware of the suffering in the world!'

'Laura, that's not true!' he said, abruptly standing up.

'Yes, it is!' With that, she stood and stormed out of the room. He could hear her determined footsteps echoing down the hall.

When dusk came, Laura had been sitting in her room for some time. Very quietly, Mrs Jones entered.

When Laura looked up, she frowned. Mrs Jones looked forlorn.

'Mrs Wesley,' she ventured, 'I have to tell you something, my lady.'

'There's a building called Morley Place on the north of this property and another one called Southeby Hall on the south end of the Manor.'

Laura sighed. *Typical*, she thought, *mansions all over the place.*

'So,' Mrs Jones continued, 'Morley Place is an institution that Sir James built for the poor. On the other side of the estate is Southeby Hall, for the ill and dying. All funded by Sir James himself. He is trying to assist the poor as much as he possibly can, but it is not easy. It has taken a toll on him.'

Laura's mouth was open and she felt regret in her stomach

growing by the minute. She had really misjudged James and she needed to apologise.

She hurried from the room and went to the main sitting room. She could see him in the gardens and rushed out to him.

She hesitated and stood a little away from him. He looked at her with sad eyes.

'James, I am so sorry I misjudged you. Mrs Jones told me about Morley Place and the other one.'

'Southeby Hall, yes,' he said and smiled. Then he looked away.

'Please forgive me. I am truly sorry for the way I spoke to you.' Laura took in a breath.

'No matter, I understand. You and I both have misgivings about aristocrats.' He sat on the garden seat by the fountain. Laura ventured forward.

'I cannot persuade the royals, or a lot of my friends, to help.' He sighed.

'Laura, I felt an urge to do something, almost as if God wanted me to. But it is extremely difficult to encourage the powers that be to even look at the problem. I nearly came to the end of my —' he hesitated, remembering when he had put a pistol to his head, 'my tether,' he said. 'People think I am odd, even insane for building Morley and Southeby. They think I will face financial ruin because of these ventures. I don't really mind, if it means something. At present, it does not.'

'We have many poor houses, but they are not to my liking as they treat the poor like criminals, well, that's my opinion anyway.'

'May I see?'

'Sorry?'

'May I see Morley Place?'

'Well, it is not a place for a woman, Laura, it would be most unwise.'

She smiled at him and came closer. 'I know,' she said and stared into his eyes.

'Well,' he said, 'if you're sure.'

'Absolutely.' She smiled.

He smiled. He felt relieved; she was so like him, her passion evident in her scolding of him when she thought of him as frivolous. Now he believed she may be warming to him.

He moved towards her, taking her hand and kissing it, while staring at her with his amazing blue eyes. Then he bowed with his left hand behind his back. She sometimes felt this gesture exciting, so she had to remind herself not to touch him. She believed he would think it improper for a lady to do so.

Chapter 10

MORLEY PLACE

The next day they set off for Morley Place by carriage. A driver and a footman accompanied them. James was dressed in a grey jacket and breeches, matching hat, white stockings and black shoes. The lace at his neck was excessive, and pinned with a silver pin. Laura, on the other hand, was dressed in a plain brown dress and a black hat. Jennifer had donated all the clothes in the Oak Room to her, stating that she had ample clothing at her own residence. At the time, Laura was annoyed but hid it well. These aristocrats had everything, too much of everything!

Morley Place was three stories high and made of sandstone. The large front door was painted black and appeared slightly battered. Upon entering Laura noticed that straw was spread on the floor, and a faint smell of urine lingered.

The first thing she saw was the children. They had fresh clothing on and shoes. They seemed clean but very thin. Some were eating bread thickly spread with butter; their mothers looked at Laura with sad eyes. Everyone was quite solemn.

James gestured and steered her towards the staircase. Laura could smell the pungent smell of urine more strongly now. In the upstairs were beds which were very low. They were simply structures to keep the occupant off the floor. The bedding was minimal.

The next floor up was much the same, many people lived here, not too cramped but all the same, not ideal. James explained there were many people in need. In the other poor houses (he stressed he never called Morley that, it was a refuge), there was the opinion that the underprivileged were poor because they were bad and therefore those that ran the houses were condescending. That was their way, that was their opinion. James saw it all in a very different light.

Then James spoke with a girl who was sitting on a bench. 'Laura, I would like you to meet Catherine.'

Catherine was petite. Dark haired and underweight. She was not easy to look at. Laura kept smiling at her so that she was at ease. Tears streamed down Catherine's face; her nose was completely missing. She put a handkerchief to her face and nodded at Laura.

'I am so pleased to meet you, Catherine.' Laura was filled with emotion.

James nodded to Catherine. 'You can trust Laura, I promise.' He wanted her to tell Laura about her life.

'I was in love with a young gentleman, he was so kind to me. I have nothing, I have always had nothing.' She suddenly looked down, ashamed of the fact. 'He put me into quarters in London and then when I was with child, I got sick.'

James looked at Laura, and simply said, 'Syphilis.'

'I had the baby,' continued Catherine, she wrung her hands, 'it was a boy, and then he died. He only lived for two days and two nights.'

'Oh, Catherine,' said Laura sadly.

James explained to Laura that the sick stayed at Southeby Hall until they recovered, then moved to Morley Place, trying to have some sort of future.

Eventually it was time for everyone to eat. Catherine as well as the others began to gather in the main dining room. Not wanting to intrude further, Laura and James went back downstairs.

James said, 'Do you know you can have holes in your head because of that treacherous disease?'

'Holes?' repeated Laura, horrified but unsure if that could be true. However, syphilitic ulceration of the scalp was indeed a fact of life.

'Yes, cupid's disease,' he said quietly. He shook his head,

knowing that the fear within his chest would rise again.

He had to admit to himself that he was deathly afraid of sexually transmitted disease. He had seen terrible examples of syphilis and so had lived a chaste life, unlike his friends and acquaintances, some of whom threw caution to the wind time and time again, and for what? Desire, not love.

He knew they mocked him and had done so relentlessly in his youth until their mutual friend Clive had caught syphilis and not only lost his nose but also his life. The ridicule stopped, although James knew they still thought him overly cautious when it came to desires of the flesh. He stood steadfast to his caution, for in his heart he knew that the only happiness one could obtain was to love someone deeply and completely forever, and one could only accomplish such a love if, in return, they loved you the same.

'Laura, perhaps I shouldn't have introduced you to Catherine. It is such a grave situation.'

'Well, I feel privileged that you let me see your work, your kindness. I am impressed.'

James held his head high. He thought, *she understands me.*

When Laura walked back down to the ground floor, James gestured to the back door and opened it. Many building materials as well as blocks of stone sat in tall piles. 'I hope to house a further sixty people here, I just have to make a start on the extension.'

'And you can supply all they need?'

'Yes. Beds, food and fresh water.'

'Do they have to work?'

'No, I have some help from the Lincolnshire doctors, they try to aid recovery. Then when some energy is restored, training takes place for a position, usually in servitude. Everyone needs a profession so as to have some control over one's life.' Laura nodded and beamed at him.

Her thoughts went to the many women she had noticed who were afflicted by syphilis in some way.

'It is just very sad how things are with that disease, when I know that penicillin eradicates it all,' she said, taking him unaware.

James said 'What is peni—'

'It doesn't matter, it would be hard for you to understand. I just wish it existed in this era.'

Laura walked on ahead of him; he hurried to catch up.

She moved around inspecting the building materials, running her hand over the smooth stone.

He watched her for a time, then came and put his fingers to her chin, lifting her face. He smiled, kissed her and said, 'I lie awake at night thinking of you and imagine what it would be like to be your loving husband.' He hesitated, then said, 'I love you, marry me. Laura, marry me.'

The intensity in his blue eyes took her breath away. Laura did not expect this and did not answer as she was shocked, not only at his words but at the way she was filled with excitement.

He grew concerned at her silence but did not press the matter. He smiled and offered her his arm, and they walked to the carriage. She was like a beautiful bird, yet he thought he may have ruined everything declaring himself too soon; she could now simply fly away. He was amazed he could not engage in other thoughts; it was all about her. How beautiful she was, but also, what a delightful person she actually appeared to be. James was in love.

They arrived at the Manor and sat together, comforted by the fire, in the drawing room where tea was served.

Their conversation was about Morley and Southeby; there was no mention of James's proposal. He grew increasingly concerned at this. He stood to be closer to the fire.

Laura noticed that James's lace was unravelling. She beckoned him to her. He noted his excitement at this development. She reached up and straightened the lace, smiling at him. 'Your lace was crooked, and you've lost your silver pin. There, that looks better.'

It was a valuable piece of jewellery, however, it was worth

the cost for the touch of this very beautiful woman. He had to steel himself and move away. It took all his strength not to take her into his arms and kiss her.

'Goodness,' said James, 'we have been chatting for ages. Please excuse me, I will see you at dinner, Laura.' He signalled to Mrs Jones who was walking down the hall.

'Mrs Jones, please take care of Mrs Wesley.'

Laura was unsure what that meant, however, Mrs Jones said, 'Would you like to retire and freshen up before dinner, my lady?'

Laura came to realise that aristocrats took a lot of time preparing for dinner.

They would change their clothes and spend hours on their appearance. Initially she thought this rather frivolous, however, she decided it was best to try and accept the way things were. The critical Laura needed to learn to compromise.

⁂

Later, Mrs Jones managed to stop Sir James in the hall. 'There's something I need to tell you, sir.'

'Yes,' James smiled at her.

She beckoned for a young girl to come forward 'This is—'

'Hannah, isn't it?' James said, priding himself on remembering her name. There were many servants at the Manor, and he believed he knew all of their names. The girl smiled grimly. She had sad brown eyes and black hair.

'She's in the family way,' Mrs Jones said.

James was surprised.

'Who is the father?' He half expected it to be Jacob; he had noticed that the young man had a soft spot for Hannah.

Margaret swallowed audibly before saying 'Sir Hugh Williams.'

James closed his eyes in disbelief and shook his head.

'And how in God's name could this happen?' James was appalled.

'Well,' Mrs Jones grew uncomfortable, 'he stayed here for three days when you were in Edinburgh with the Earl of Berrisfordshire.'

Realisation came to James like a slap in the face. He was horrified. 'You're telling me he forcibly took Hannah, against her will, while under my roof, is that correct?' He moved his hands around vigorously.

Mrs Jones nodded.

'This is treachery of the worst kind!' Then James looked at Mrs Jones intensely, 'And why, Margaret, did you not tell me that he had stayed in my home?'

'He asked me not to mention it to you, sir. I now see why, or rather when Hannah told me he—'

'For goodness' sake!'

James was somewhat flustered and began bellowing for Henry.

Henry came hurriedly and looked rather concerned.

'Henry, Hugh Williams is never to be allowed to stay at Harrington Manor in my absence ever again, is that clear?' Henry, blinking rapidly, nodded, then looked perplexed. Surely James knew that he as a servant could never stop an aristocrat such as Sir Hugh Williams from doing exactly what he wanted to do.

James looked thoughtful. 'We must take care of Hannah, you know what to do, Margaret, Dr Stevenson should be informed.' Then he added, 'All expenses to me.'

Mrs Jones felt very much relieved. Hannah was pleased. Mrs Jones had assured her that Sir James would allow her to stay at the Manor.

As James regained his composure he said, 'Mrs Jones,' he paused, smiled, 'Margaret, I would be obliged if you didn't mention this to Mrs Wesley.'

'Very good, sir.'

James watched the two women walk down the hall. He felt guilty that this had happened, but also wanted to keep it from Laura. She may agree to marry him, and this could jeopardise his chance at happiness.

Chapter 11

THE DECISION

Eventually James and Laura sat down to dine. James was dressed above and beyond anything Laura could call formal wear. He was turned out from top to toe in what looked like blue satin, with heavy embroidery and lace at the neck. He always tied his hair back with a black ribbon, however, this evening it was blue velvet.

As they finished their dessert, Laura said, 'James, there is a gap of almost two hundred and sixty years between us. I don't think it could work.'

She did not need to elaborate, he knew exactly what she was referring to, his proposal of wedlock.

Her words cut him, however he recovered enough to say, 'Well, don't decide just yet, think about it.' He smiled although he did not feel anything that would warrant a smile. 'Let's have a cup of tea.'

The logic of Laura's rejection was understandable but

it hurt him; he really did love her without doubt. James excused himself and said he would return shortly, he needed to think.

Laura retired to the drawing room, enjoying the warmth of the fire. She thought about James, how she enjoyed his company and was indeed flattered at the proposal. He was so courageous and so handsome. The state of the world in 1765 had a lot about it that was negative. There was more to consider besides the excitement of living at the Manor with a handsome aristocrat.

Did she love him, or did she just think she did?

Just then James appeared. His face was ashen, and he stepped in front of her.

'Laura, I wish to withdraw my proposal of marriage. It was very selfish of me. I understand that in your era, in the future, there is great development and that there will be many things you would have that I cannot give you. Forgive me if I caused you any distress.'

He bowed and retreated through the huge double doors that led to the hall.

Laura felt sad. *Are you falling in love with him,* she asked herself. However, she did not know the answer. She shook her head; it could not possibly work.

Meanwhile, James went out to the stables and mounted Captain. He rode out to the cliffs and mulled over the disaster that was before him. She had stirred his heart, but he could not have her.

The next morning, James and Laura sat down to breakfast. After Laura had picked at her meal, she said, 'Sir James, I have decided to go home, I think it's the right thing to do.'

He felt like a knife had pierced him. This love was so powerful but it was not to be. The crushing blow was she had referred to him as sir, when earlier she had agreed to call him James. Already she was slipping away from him, and he knew that a love such as this was rare, never to be repeated. He had never felt this way about anyone, ever!

What was he to do? It would be selfish to marry her, and now it would be difficult not to see her every day. Then he had to face the fact that she may not have feelings for him. *I had moved too fast*, he thought. If only there had been more time, they could have perhaps developed a friendship; that would have pleased him immensely.

Not looking at her, he said, 'Very well, I have to travel to London this morning. It is a long journey and I have a business meeting tomorrow. I shan't see you again, so I wish you all the very best.' He then stared at her, his face a picture of sadness.

'I wish you well also, and thank you for everything,' Laura managed.

'God speed,' he said. He stood up, bowed and was gone.

Somehow his bow did not fill her with excitement; she would miss him.

She stood before the mirror in her room. *I can't stay*, she thought, *I can't, I must go home!*

Laura did not say anything to Mrs Jones about leaving. In the morning, the kindly servant had brought tea and a bowl with bread, milk and sugar to her bedroom. Afterwards, Laura sat for a very long time at the large glass-paned doors. The Manor was very quiet. Eventually, she lay on the bed and quietly slipped away.

When she opened her eyes, she was in her home. It was dark and she was on her bed. In the distance there was the sound of traffic. *What day was it?* She had no idea. The house was quiet, empty and cold. Laura felt a deep sense of ... loneliness.

After a long, hot shower, the one thing very much missed, she smiled. Jacob would be bringing hot water for her bath, and Mrs Jones would be wondering where Laura had got to.

Watching TV, learning how things had progressed without

her, she channel-hopped for a while and charged her phone, which was full of adverts, scam emails and, surprisingly, not many text messages or missed calls. The mail was equally uninteresting, however a court notification had come that Edward Richards was convicted of vehicular homicide. The sentence was four years. Four years for a life; it didn't seem right somehow. What was Dan's life worth? Surely more. She had not attended court, and it filled her with regret.

She could live without all the mod cons of this life, even the money did not mean much to her. Thinking that maybe 1765 wasn't so bad after all, she shook her head, it wasn't 1765 that mattered, it was James.

Laura called the professor to see how things had been while she was away.

'Where have you been?' The professor was delighted to hear from her and insisted she come to visit him immediately.

'Yes, of course, I'm on my way,' she said.

They sat drinking tea and Laura told him everything of her adventure.

'I have to tell you; I think I am in love with James and I am tempted to return to him. But how can I live in James's world? No internet, no mobile phone, no TV, no running water or electricity, no shopping online,' her eyes widened, 'no cars! Oh God!'

'Love conquers all,' said the professor, amused.

'I don't think so!' said Laura.

'Are you sure?' He smiled widely. 'Are you certain you will not be returning to him and his less than perfect world?'

Laura gave out a frustrated noise and threw her hands in the air vigorously. She had made up her mind she would not return to Harrington Manor. She would have to live without that dashing, handsome, kind man.

Chapter 12

HARRINGTON MANOR

James sat by the open, glass-paned doors of his bedroom in the semi-darkness. He had moved his things back that day, only to feel so foreign in his own room, as it had been hers.

The locket he had given her was on the table. He picked it up, holding it fondly.

He thought, *I am brave but miserable. I am destined to love and love deeply, sadly I cannot succeed. Can I live without love?* He shook his head, *I am being unreasonable; I should be grateful for what I have.*

The peacock came to the open doors. He approached James hesitantly. Laura had begun to feed the birds. Mrs Jones giving her a bowl of grain every day.

'Laura isn't here,' he paused, 'she is never coming back.'

The peacock, as though he understood, slowly moved on.

James sat in silence trying to reflect. Much time passed.

I need to be strong, less emotional, he thought.

He was suddenly aware that someone was in the room. He looked up, shocked. At first they just looked at each other, then he stood up.

Laura felt tears sting her eyes. 'I can't live without you,' she whispered.

'Oh, my darling!' He held out his arms to her. She ran to him, he kissed her, holding her for a very long time.

Eventually, he said, 'Everything will be alright.'

He realised he should give up his bedroom again. It was only right that she should have the most opulent room in the Manor. *How wonderful*, he thought, *Laura came back to me.*

⁂

The next day Mrs Jones found James sitting in the drawing room. 'How are you this morning, sir?'

James looked thoughtful and said, 'That wonderful person who I believed would not marry me, has agreed to be my wife. Happiness is too small a word to describe how elated I am.' He looked into the distance, contented.

'I am so pleased!'

Mrs Jones noticed James had become exuberant of late, able to show his emotions more. He was no longer forlorn, dejected, docile.

'Thank you, Margaret,' James said, smiling at her. 'Do you know where Mrs Wesley has got to?'

'She is with Peter,' she said, busying herself with tidying.

'Peter?'

'My lady has named one of the peacocks Peter, sir.'

He found Laura in the gardens and watched her feed grain to the eager bird.

'I believe this is Peter!' he said, laughing.

They walked towards Laura's room, and she took his hand, bringing him inside from the garden, and closed the doors.

She hugged him and kissed him passionately. He took hold of her, excited, feeling he had to have her, but his religious self objected. He towered over her; her eyes closed.

You are so — different,' he whispered. He pressed against her.

Then he said, 'I can't,' trying to free himself from her arms.

'What do you mean?' she said, puzzled.

He lifted her to him, they kissed again. She gave herself up to him willingly, touching him everywhere, igniting him further. Finally, he managed to break away from her.

'What's wrong?' Laura was bewildered.

'I have to preserve your virtuous self, my dear, it would not be right for me to proceed.' He was almost breathless.

Laura was expressionless and then whispered, 'I can do

this without the wedding cake.'

He closed his eyes and shook his head.

'Right,' she said and not looking back, left the room.

James opened his eyes trying to regain his composure. He was hopelessly in love with her, but they were not yet married, they must wait. Once married, they could become lovers. Her reputation was extremely important to him.

James went outside, saddled up Captain and rode over to the Ashcroft Tavern. He just wanted to be away from the Manor, in order to think. He ordered a cognac which he drank quickly.

His religion had saved him from debauchery, from the disease of giving into sexual desires. He felt muddled; he ordered another drink. He should go to church tomorrow, perhaps it would sooth his soul. He knew she was chaste, but her reputation must remain intact.

The next morning, when James returned from church, he found Laura in the main drawing room and took hold of both her hands. 'My darling,' he said. She smiled at him, and he thought he had been forgiven for yesterday.

She was wearing Jennifer's pink dress, the one with the embroidered bodice, and although it covered everything, it accentuated her womanly attributes, making her more desirable than ever.

Somehow the dress was not wide, not like other women's

dresses.

He noticed how her eyelashes were lengthy and that there was a small predominant freckle on the right side of her face, near her ear. She was such a natural beauty. She did not need help from accessories, as he had come to think of them. Extra hair with pearls attached. Feathers that seemed so long, they were a vexation to one's eyes. Laura is just a very beautiful woman, and that was that. The nakedness of her face made him think of her naked, though he didn't mean to. He felt his religious self suddenly crumple under the desire that rose within. He was so in love with her. That previous evening when he was alone, on and on he had thought of her appeal, was he obsessed?

Later that afternoon, James sat in the library writing letters. He could hear Laura calling the name Maggie over and over again. She was somewhere in the gardens.

Mrs Jones was tidying books on a shelf when James asked, 'Mrs Jones, who is Maggie?'

'Grey stray cat,' said Mrs Jones, continuing on with her cleaning.

James frowned.

'Taken in by Mrs Wesley. She named it after me, sir.'

'I should have known.' *My future wife is a kind soul*, he thought.

He smiled to himself while returning to his correspondence. Seeing that he needed more paper, he opened the desk drawer and found a long-forgotten note he had penned to the king. It had never been sent, as the king had unexpectedly visited James the following day.

The monarch, by way of courier, had sent a letter asking James why his dear friend had built Morley Place and Southeby Hall. George was concerned that James may face financial ruin because of this venture. It was a friendly query but still a query. Benevolence towards the poor was not something royalty thought much about.

James had responded and now read his reply.

Your Majesty,

I am forever England. Should I die this very day, I smile contented in the belief that this land, its people and its future are very much assured.

I have endeavoured to change despair to contented existence. That, my never-ending quest. God bless the poor, the sick, and keep them safe.

Thank you for your concern sire, however, I am steadfast to my quest.

Your humble servant,

Sir James Harrington, Baronet

Chapter 13

THE DINNER PARTY

James decided to have a dinner party, only inviting a small number of people so that Laura would feel comfortable. He needed to introduce her to his acquaintances so that when they married, no one would be surprised.

His heart would pound when he thought about her becoming Lady Harrington. It seemed unbelievable. He had not made any arrangements as yet but knew his future was assured, with her as his wife. He would tingle at the thought and have to close his eyes and think of something else as a distraction.

On the day of the gathering, Laura allowed Mrs Jones to attach bits and pieces to her hair so that it grew in height. Feathers and pearls completed the crown effect, which was all the rage in society. Laura had allowed some colour to be applied to her cheeks and lips but nothing too drastic. Mrs Jones was slightly disappointed at the understated look.

A special dress had been made, but Laura had insisted on only a small, flared petticoat. She also wore the locket that James had given her.

On the evening of the event, James came upon her in the hall. He was transfixed.

Knowing he adored her, Laura was fascinated by the fact that he always seemed to be mesmerised when she appeared. He would stare at her with such love in his eyes, it was at times astonishing.

She smiled at him, 'I look ridiculous.' She touched her exaggerated hairdo.

'Not to me,' he said quite seriously, 'you are very beautiful.'

'I am very nervous; I am not used to this sort of thing.'

'You will be alright, just try to relax darling.'

She smiled, comforted.

The gala event was spectacular. James made sure that every detail was seen to. Fifty people attended and were seated in the Green Room, which had in the past accommodated over one hundred comfortably. The enormous paintings that hung in gold frames, along with the soft green walls, made the room very attractive, although to Laura's mind it was a little ostentatious. Ever since she had arrived, she and James had eaten their meals there.

Laura made up her mind to be less critical as, by marrying

James, she would become one of them, an aristocrat. She would therefore need to be adaptable.

This evening it was uncertain if King George would make an appearance, though the guests were suitably impressed that the monarch was actually a friend of their host.

George was devoted to his wife, Charlotte, and James was greatly impressed by this and knew the king felt disappointed with some of his cohorts for their lack of morals.

On occasion, invitations to palace functions were sent to Harrington Manor. The two also spent many a pleasant afternoon playing chess when James was in London. There were also a few times the king had arrived at the Manor without warning, the servants delighted but also fearful of putting a foot wrong. The king had a habit of wandering around the Manor unannounced, startling staff and smiling as he proceeded from room to room. 'Good morning, ladies,' he would call as the servants scrambled to line up and curtsy.

Often, he would end up, of all places, in the kitchen and partake in a cup of tea before Sir James, learning of his arrival, came to greet him.

It was thought King George rather enjoyed the scurrying effect he had on the servants.

James was very pleased with how Laura had been accepted by his friends and acquaintances. He was also glad George had not been able to attend; Laura would have been very nervous to meet the King of England.

Jennifer, who was dressed in a very wide dress, exaggerated hair, pearls, feathers and long white gloves, had gravitated to Laura and became excited about introducing her to the other ladies, whose wide dresses rustled as they moved.

If truth be told, they all felt superior because of Laura's modest look, but they also admired her beauty. Jennifer managed to briefly introduce Nicholas, Lord Lawrence, to Laura, then whisked her away for more introductions.

Sir Hugh Williams paraded around smiling at everyone. He wore a green jacket with gold buttons, matching breeches, grey stockings and black shoes.

He had on a white shirt with lace at the neck and had donned a powdered wig with fashionable side curls that somehow made his plump face more predominant.

Some time back, Hugh had been a delightful fellow and a good friend to James, Nicholas and Nigel. They were inseparable; experiencing the wonderful days of youth, adventure and prosperity. The dear friends revelled in the thrill of striking out on their own as young men, celebrating their good fortune and good looks, and experiencing life to the fullest.

Then one day, Hugh met Jane. His three friends excitedly

awaited the announcement that Jane Hammond would marry Hugh, who frequently bought her expensive jewellery and presents during his business trips to Paris.

James, a man who never experienced envy, at that time felt the pang of it.

When the joyous event never happened, Hugh sank into alcoholism.

Jane had been secretly seeing another man; one that was extremely handsome, wealthier than Hugh and besotted. When he proposed, she had discarded Hugh.

He saw Jane now, far across the room, and his heart almost stopped.

She looked at him with disdain and it cut him to ribbons. He cursed himself for still having feelings for her. He gulped down his port and continued drinking heavily until he happened to see Laura standing alone.

Hugh came to her and leaning in very close, his alcoholic breath pungent, he whispered, 'What does a man have to part with to have you visit for a pleasant afternoon, eh? I have some good gin to share.' Laura looked at him with contempt. 'I would never have a drink with you, never.' The gossip about Sir Hugh, at the Manor, was extremely negative.

Also, Laura was now totally detached from alcohol and did not like to be around those who wished to be intoxicated.

He had a faint smile as he bowed and left her side. *Clever little whore*, he thought.

Hugh's habit of excessive alcohol consumption had put a slight damper on things. He had ambled over to James and asked about Laura, in a less than decent way, insinuating that she was perhaps available for his amusement.

James had responded solemnly, 'Mrs Wesley is a widow. There was an accident while I was riding, I caused her great harm. She is my guest. If you do not desist from this line of inference, I shall take the matter further, sir.' James stared at him coldly.

'I am deathly afraid of that!' Hugh said and laughed. He felt James had become a weak man and always seemed to be emotionally driven, rather than strong. He was too kind for his own good. Surely the poor and the needy took advantage of him.

Sir Hugh prided himself on being stern. The lower classes did not make eye contact with him, and he rejoiced in their respect, even though it was through fear. *Fear is a good thing*, he thought.

'Farewell, my friend,' he said to James, who gave him a blank look; it was neither threatening nor friendly. Hugh pointed a finger at him, 'I shall see you by the by,' and he was gone, in search of more alcohol.

Chapter 14

THE PHEASANT SHOOT

One crisp morning, Nigel, Hugh and Nicholas came to Harrington Manor for a pheasant shoot. The servants Henry, Gerald and Jacob stood by to do whatever was required by the gentry. Six springer spaniels came with Lord Lawrence, all brown and white with eager eyes. Nicholas was a tall, handsome man with black hair and green eyes. He dressed exceptionally well, a lot like James.

James never killed anything, just wanted to spend time with his friends. If truth be told, he didn't particularly care for the taste of pheasant although he knew Mrs Jones would be pleased to get the birds and roast them in the Harrington Manor ovens. He was not in a good mood and the gunfire only made things worse. The sun was very bright, the sky clear. The others were happily chatting, enjoying the day. The shoot was successful, and the birds frequently plummeted to the ground, only to be gathered up by the excited dogs who raced back to the men. After a while, the men took a break and drams of brandy were shared around, along with pleasant banter.

Hugh Williams, with his reputation as the local drunk and philanderer, only added to James's displeasure. Hugh looked rather dishevelled, was under the influence of gin and was being very loud. Nigel purposely moved away from him, annoyed.

It was then that the fateful incident occurred.

Williams moved, almost stumbling, towards James, and took hold of his arm to steady himself.

'That woman you have tucked away at the Manor. Send her over to me, I can give her a good shilling or two.'

James recognised the insinuation. Seething, he suddenly pushed Hugh in the chest, who stumbled back. James pushed him again and again until Hugh grabbed at Nigel for balance. 'You have slandered the lady's name. I cannot have that!' His blue eyes menacing.

Hugh raised his eyebrows, surprised.

'I demand an apology!'

'For that? She doesn't even know how to dress; she is no lady.' Hugh wobbled about. 'I will not apologise, this is absurd!' He reached deep into his pocket and raised a bottle of Greenall's Gin to his lips and drank. 'You're not serious!'

he said, waving his hand about, grinning.

'Do I not look serious? I demand a duel, Hugh. As the challenger I suggest swords, I shall see you at Hatherleigh Hall at six o'clock in the morning, along with your seconds,' he paused, 'I bid you farewell,' he said bitterly. He began to walk.

'Are you mad, you must see that she is a whore!' Williams shouted angrily at the top of his voice. Everyone froze with horror.

James stopped, as though he had been physically struck, shocked at the words. He did not retaliate; he would seek retribution in the morning, Laura's honour must be defended. He began to walk again.

Nigel and Nicholas shook their heads at each other. The servants stood with concerned faces, not knowing what to do next. Nigel tapped Hugh on the shoulder, 'Come on, you better go home.'

Lord Lawrence, cousin to James, was rather surprised at the turn of events. Hatherleigh Hall was his home. Of course, he would never deny a family member access, but he was concerned about the possible loss of life, also the rumours that would undoubtably ensue.

Chapter 15

THE DUEL

The gentle rain fell as James rode up to Hatherleigh Hall on Captain, Nigel following in a carriage. The grass was lush, glistening wet and slippery.

The atmosphere was deathly quiet, no bird song. Some of the Harrington Manor servants had come to watch and were sheltering in the doorway of a barn. Two of the women, upset, were crying without making a sound. Sir James could die, and what would become of them?

The seconds were a gentleman named Thomas Evans standing for Hugh Williams, and on behalf of James, who else but his best friend, Nigel Matthews.

James who had taken an early morning bath and had shaved was wearing a white shirt, grey pants and black boots.

A dishevelled Williams on the other hand was dressed in a creased grey jacket, brown shirt and pants. He wore black boots and was not entirely sober, whereas James had no drink in him.

Nigel came to James, concerned. 'Can I not talk you out of this, James?'

'Absolutely not.'

'Then I shall check the weapons and stand by to see all is fair.'

'Thank you.'

Eventually, both opponents stood opposite each other, swords in hand.

Nigel, as James's second, stood facing both men. 'Gentlemen, can you desist and resolve your conflict without bloodshed?' There was no answer.

Dr Stevenson, burdened with the task of observer, stood stony-faced looking at the men intently.

And so, the duel commenced.

Alertness engulfed James, his concentration sharp, and with his left hand at his waist, a typical duelist stance, he thrust forward at Hugh, who moved around parrying. Eventually, Hugh had the upper hand and stabbed at James who, light on his feet, easily stepped away. He then nodded at Hugh who quickened the pace and lunged forward. Their swords moved back and forth, the sound cutting the stillness of the morning. Nigel became very concerned at the intensity of the conflict, it was not the intention to murder, but to wound. Both men introduced more power into their moves. Suddenly James tripped and fell. Hugh smiled.

Chapter 16

AN INCORRECT ASSUMPTION

Laura had just completed breakfast. There seemed to be less staff than usual.

'Henry, where is Sir James?'

'He's at Hatherleigh Hall partaking in a duel.'

'What?'

'Yes, my lady, on your behalf; he is defending your honour.'

'Defending my honour? What on earth does that mean?'

Henry was loathed to explain and simply said 'I am sure he will be home directly, my lady.'

Laura felt her heart racing, her hands shaking.

She kept looking out of the large front windows, but there was no sign of James. The rain persisted; the Manor was unusually quiet. *Where were the servants*?

Suddenly she could hear something faint in the distance. A carriage was coming but she could not see James riding

Captain, and she felt uneasy.

Closer and closer the carriage came and suddenly it was by the front windows. As it passed, she saw Captain tied to the back. It could only mean one thing: *he's dead*, she thought, and with that, she sank to the floor.

They would be coming to tell her he was dead.

The footsteps in the hall grew louder, and she was filled with terror. She closed her eyes tightly and heard the double doors bang open. She could hear the heavy tread of boots coming closer and was stunned when James said, 'Why Laura, whatever is the matter?' He took hold of her and drew her up to him.

'I thought you were dead.' She could hardly stand and rested against him.

'My dear,' he hesitated, he was pained to explain a very delicate occurrence to her. Finally, he said 'I cannot allow anyone to make offensive comments about you.' He stared into her eyes. 'You are to be my wife, Lady Harrington. All and sundry will respect you, or answer to me!' His eyes flashed, his manner stern.

When he saw her distress, he softened and said, 'It's the way things are here. You need to accept my wisdom, Laura.' Moving away from her, he straightened and lifted his chin. He was proud of what he had done.

'What comments?'

'Hugh Williams provoked me with his inflammatory remarks about my future wife, I do not wish to repeat them to you.' He paused for a moment then said, 'I cannot let that sort of thing go.' He moved to the windows to gaze out at the rain.

Laura stared after him. 'Did you kill him?' she said in a small voice.

James turned and looked at her.

He had managed to avoid everything Hugh tried to do. Even when he tripped, he was able to dash away gathering momentum. Finally, James had put his adversary on the ground, kicking away his sword. Mrs Jones was frozen with dread when James held his own sword to the man's throat.

Hugh thought, *I deserve this; I am a despicable person.* There were tears in his eyes, but he summoned the courage to lift his head and look his opponent in the eye. James hesitated and then said, 'I need you to leave and never return. I will spare you injury Hugh, but if I see your face again, I will resume this dispute, I give you my word!'

Nigel had drawn Williams up to his feet, then Thomas put him into a waiting carriage.

'Nigel,' James had called, 'get Captain and tie him to the back of the carriage, I will ride home with you,' he sighed heavily, wiping the sweat from his brow and tucking a strand of blond hair back in place. Nigel, putting his hand on his friend's back, nodded. Both seconds, as well as Dr Stevenson, attested to the fact that there was no damage to either duellist. The matter was closed and many of the common folk of Lincolnshire later spread rumours far and wide that Sir James Harrington was a hero, that Sir Hugh Williams was a cad, a wicked man who deserved his comeuppance, and that he had been ordered to leave Lincolnshire, never to return. This news delighted many residents.

James's thoughts were brought back when Laura pressed, 'Well, did you kill him?'

'I didn't extinguish his life, my dear. I merely requested that he leave the area, so that I, for one, do not have to deal with him again.' He said this rather triumphantly with a smile, he felt good.

'Do you engage in duels frequently?' she asked, distressed.

'No, no. Laura please!' he protested. 'I was involved in only one other duel, when I was younger, twenty-one. Other than that, no.'

'So, you let that person go free too, like today, like Hugh?'

James did not speak right away, then said 'No, I killed him.'

Laura was shocked.

'Look, I don't think you understand these types of situations, it is difficult to explain.'

'Right,' she said, 'I think I will go to my room.'

'My room,' he smiled, trying to make light of the situation.

She stared at him wide-eyed.

'Sorry,' he said and bowed, one hand behind his back. He had picked up that this gesture of courtesy pleased her. Only today it had no effect.

James smiled at Laura and pulled the bellpull wherein Henry appeared.

'I want morning tea served. I shall just clean up.'

'Very good, sir,' said Henry.

James turned to face Laura and bowed again. 'My dear,' he said, 'I shall see you shortly,' and strode from the room. Nigel, who was waiting in the hall, smiled warmly at James and they walked together.

When Laura returned to her room, a pensive Margaret Jones came to her and whispered, 'My lady, I have to tell you something.'

Laura was concerned; the servant was always very helpful, especially when she had thought James was a self-centred man. How wrong she had been then, so on this occasion, she was very attentive.

'Go on,' Laura said.

With great trepidation, Mrs Jones said, 'You seem upset because in his younger days Sir James killed Thomas Henley.'

'Thomas Henley?'

Mrs Jones nodded. 'The gentleman was killing people, my lady, women.'

Mrs Jones nodded and waited to see if this shocked Laura.

'What did the law do about it?'

Mrs Jones shook her head sadly.

'Sir James insulted him and there was a duel, so that was the end of it, my lady.'

Laura sat open-mouthed.

'Thanks be to God,' added Mrs Jones.

She motioned to Laura with her hand. 'He did it for the good of us common folk.'

Laura was uneasy because yet again she had judged so quickly, without question, and how wrong she had been.

James was in the stables talking with Nigel and Jacob when he noticed her approach. Pleasantly surprised, he smiled warmly. Jacob begun to brush Captain and James held out his hand. She put her hand on top, as was the custom. They walked outside.

'I am coming in for tea, I just wanted to check on Captain.'

Laura nodded. 'I wish to apologise,' she stated.

'Apologise?' he said.

She noticed his amazing eyes; so blue, so kind.

'I heard about Thomas Henley; I am sorry, I didn't realise.'

'Realise what?'

'That Thomas needed to —go away,' she hesitated, 'permanently.'

James nodded, then his face was sad.

He leant forward and whispered in her ear, 'There was no other way.'

He suddenly brightened. 'Come, let's have a cup of tea.'

Laura, her hand still on top of his, squeezed his affectionately.

As they walked, she asked, 'Why didn't the law do something?'

James stopped and very seriously said, 'The domination of evil men with power and connections.'

As they walked on, James said, 'I yearn for a world such as yours Laura, where money isn't dominant in life, and all people are considered equal.'

Laura frowned. Her society still favoured the rich, but equality was more of a reality there than here in 1765.

Chapter 17

VISITING FRIENDS

The following Wednesday, the weather being mild, Laura and James had decided to visit Nigel and Jennifer.

Laura had been taking an early morning walk in the gardens when she happened upon the stables. Finding Captain, she admired his fine, glistening body and nuzzled him. He responded in kind.

James, delighted to see her, strolled over, amused. He smiled at her, 'You're stealing his heart as well as mine.'

She looked up at him with such adoration, his heart raced. He composed himself. *She loves me as I her*, he thought. *Life will be wonderful from hereon in.*

He offered her his arm. She smiled.

Jennifer, as usual, had spent all morning on her appearance. Laura's eyes took in her crown-styled hair as well as the feathers, which seemed to never end.

Jennifer noticed and said, 'Do you like my feathers? I am so in love with them.'

'They are rather— extraordinary.'

Jennifer touched Laura's arm. 'You know my lady's maid and I can help you achieve the same.'

James cleared his throat, knowing that Laura found the look rather ridiculous. 'Well, I would like a cup of tea, what?'

The four enjoyed their morning tea with sandwiches and cake.

It was later in the day when James sat with Laura after they had dinner, and a long conversation ensued about London. Laura had commenced reading a history book about the city. She had found it in the library. James, Nigel and Jennifer delighted in purchasing everything and anything their hearts desired in the city; however, the city was a grim place.

It was difficult to learn, but Laura was always one who embraced the truth, and learn she did, that London in some areas was overflowing with sewage in the streets. Sad, desolate people loitered around every corner, and a large amount of illness and death was evident. It was a cesspit and she thought it should be avoided at all costs. She reflected on the shocking facts she had learnt and decided the best thing she could do was assist James in helping the poor in Lincolnshire. London was a problem that at this point in time seemed insurmountable. This fact greatly upset her, as it had James.

She said, 'This era is so brutal, so uneven. People are very rich or very poor.'

James frowned. 'I am trying to change that. You understand me, with you by my side, we can accomplish great things, Laura.'

James and Laura spent a lot of time at Morley and Southeby. Although sometimes it was sad, they felt they were making headway. Laura began to brighten; she felt she was achieving something worthwhile. She knew she could not change history, but it was alright to help others change things. Especially miserable situations at Morley and Southeby. The people were so desperate for help, and James was trying to respond in the best way he could.

The children began to look healthier, and the women afflicted by syphilis took great comfort in their safe haven. James had explained they never had to leave but were to enjoy his hospitality indefinitely. It was a great relief to people without a future in London's judgemental society.

Marseille soap was ordered from Paris in large quantities because Laura insisted James instructed everyone to wash their hands regularly and take baths, although at times it was difficult to perform this new habit.

Chapter 18

A SHOCKING REVELATION

It was on a cool but sunny day that Laura and James were walking in the gardens of Harrington Manor, when James spoke of their future.

'Well, I think we should get married next month. The weather should be nice, and Nigel and Jennifer will be here, not dashing around Paris shopping,' he laughed. 'I cherish my best friend immensely; he and Jennifer need to be here to see us marry.

'Are you aged about nineteen, my dear?'

Laura was surprised. 'No,' she said, 'I'm twenty-four.'

He raised his eyebrows.

'Why, do you prefer a younger woman?' she teased.

He rolled his eyes thinking of Genevieve. His darling Laura was exquisite by comparison. He kissed her hand.

She said tentatively, 'The thing I am not sure about is seeing all those people at the wedding, and then there's the dancing.'

'Dancing?'

'In my society, we dance very primitively and without order.' She smiled. 'I am so afraid of making you look bad.'

'You will be alright. I can keep the wedding small, and I shall delight in teaching you how we dance. It will be wonderful, I can picture it all now.'

She was reassured and smiled at him.

Thinking of how Mary Elizabeth had criticised the Manor, James asked, 'Is there anything you would like changed in our home?'

'I love the house— mansion.'

'Do you really?' he smiled.

'Yes, I love the colour scheme and the um— candles and—'

James laughed. 'How could you possibly love candles!' he said energetically, when in your era, you have told me, you have instant light. You know, I can hardly imagine such a thing, it must be so convenient!'

Laura nodded. 'Along with the internet, mobile phones, computers, laptops and TV shows with lots of adverts, you never have a moment's peace.'

'I do not understand any of that, but I take it you love being here without all that progress.'

'Yes, you could say that.'

'It sounds to me,' James bowed, 'that your new world is

somewhat overwhelming.'

Laura sighed. 'Yes, it is. Of course, it's a world of good and bad just like here; however, you have such quiet. I am not familiar with that, although also here, there are many frightening things. I do not know what I am saying, and I know you will never understand.' She did not know how to express her alarm at the poverty and inequality she had learnt of in London.

'It is true I may not understand, but always know I wish to protect you from whatever frightens you.'

He knew that in the future, most people had rights, that was his understanding of it from their lengthy conversations. However, in 1765, royalty and the rich had all the power; Laura found this repulsive. He would have to tread carefully with her, even though he delighted in the fact she loved him. *She could give up and go back and then*, he thought, *my life will be plunged into misery again.*

It was then that she touched him affectionately, and they walked towards the Rose Garden.

'Then we will have lots of children and live happily together.' James reflected.

Laura abruptly stopped. James looked back at her inquiringly.

'I should have told you— I'm sorry, I mean I didn't think,

I'm so stupid!' she wailed loudly.

'What's wrong?' he said, puzzled.

The gardeners all stopped trimming the maze and looked up.

Noticing this, James whispered, 'Laura, you are going to be Lady Harrington, please!'

He drew her deep into the Rose Garden, away from view.

'James, I cannot have children, I don't know why I didn't say, I guess it never occurred to me!' she said anxiously. 'When I married Dan, we tried for a baby. I cannot get pregnant, it is just— not possible.'

'Rubbish, it was Daniel's fault.'

Laura looked shocked.

'I mean, it is not you. I am young and fertile, we will have children.' he said earnestly.

Laura became very upset; she knew from her consultation with the reproductive endocrinologist it was impossible.

Seeing the definite expression on her face, James said, 'You never thought to mention it to me?' He was shocked.

'There is adoption.'

'What's that?' he asked, frowning.

Then Laura realised that adoption probably did not exist in 1765 so she said, 'Nothing,' and shook her head.

The silence grew between them.

Laura said in desperation, 'Say something!'

'I am rendered speechless,' he said, his very blue eyes larger than usual.

He saw the hurt in her face and wanted to reach out to her but didn't. She stepped away and ran back to the Manor.

Laura felt great despair. James needed an heir to continue his position in society and secure the prosperity of Harrington Manor.

She sat in her room but did not open the large glass doors. Henry had come and told her that dinner would be served shortly. She did not wish to eat but thought she should make an appearance. She had thought what to say and had to face it.

James was sullen and did not look at her when she was seated at the table.

He passed a bowl of vegetable soup to her, and she placed it carefully in front of her.

'I think I should go home in the morning, then you can find a wife who can carry on the Harrington name, and I will become a distant memory.' She said this with no malice, it was just a fact, the right thing to do, to say.

'We part yet again!' said James bitterly.

'Thank you for all your kindness,' and without trying to be mean she added, 'Sir.' She smiled thinly and left the table.

By morning she was greatly recovered, and her only

thought was to go home. Harrington Manor was ostentatious, her Melbourne home more relaxed. She would miss the people at Southeby and Morley, as well as all the servants at Harrington Manor. But in time, James would have a new wife and he would forget all about her. It was for the best.

Besides, she could now enjoy all the comforts of her modern world. To her surprise, she had not missed the technology at all, but some of the comforts that eased life would be welcome. Hot running water, electricity and the freedom to express yourself. She was always concerned she might say the wrong thing and embarrass James. Some of the people in 1765 could be so judgemental and stiff. But through all these thoughts, she knew she loved him deeply and would have given anything to be his wife. But it was not to be.

James had not slept well. He had eaten breakfast alone. He had momentarily had the frightening thought that Laura had already gone, however, he heard her voice in the hall speaking with Margaret.

He was sad. She, no doubt, was upset with him, and he did not know how to undo it. He grew agitated about the whole situation.

Later, as he stood by the fire in the main drawing room, Henry came into the room.

'I am leaving shortly for a business meeting with the Earl;

would you please inform Mrs Wesley I would prefer it if she didn't disappear whilst I am gone!' he said curtly and snatching up his hat and gloves from the small cabinet by the door, walked down the hall to the front door.

'Yes, sir,' said Henry, although James was too far away to hear.

When James returned to Harrington Manor at midday, he was full of regret at how he had spoken to Laura.

He hurried into the Manor and seeing Henry, passed him his hat and gloves. 'Where is she?' he said.

'In the main drawing room I believe, sir.'

James briskly walked down the hall and entered the drawing room. Not seeing her, he said, 'She's—' but did not finish the dreadful phrase for fear it would kill him.

He ran to her room, throwing open the door and calling her name. The stillness of the room struck him. The large glass-paned doors were open, and the hypnotic scent of roses only made him feel more desolate. He proceeded to check everywhere in the Manor, calling her name over and over again to no avail. Servants who were dusting and polishing furniture scrambled to get out of his way.

Finally, he went into the gardens and yet again she was nowhere to be seen. He was filled with fear. 'She's gone,' he said aloud. He leant up against the wall for much needed support, his heart racing.

It was then that Laura walked out from the maze.

He was astonished. He ran to her and scooped her up in his arms. 'I thought you had gone!'

'Henry told me I should stay.'

He could see she was unhappy.

'Please forgive me my hesitation, I love you dearly and want you to be my wife. Nothing else matters.'

'But you need an heir.'

'No, no, I don't,' he paused, 'I only need you.' He kissed her. It began to rain, and he took her arm, bringing her indoors and shutting the door forcefully.

Laura had been hurt; he had not received the news well of her inability to give him children, not that she could blame him. That this era was hard for her to accept, with the way things were, greatly weighed on her.

They were in the drawing room now, and Laura said, 'Your world is gracious,' she paused and looked at him, 'well-mannered, and also cruel. The way people live is frightening, it would be extremely difficult for me to stay, I— I have come to realise that now.' She felt emotional.

'I will protect you always, as I did with my life. I would stake anything and everything I have to keep you safe, I love you!' he said anxiously.

Laura had moved to the divan and picked up the history book she had been reading. She suddenly was annoyed.

'Then when your love of me fades, are you going to the ladies on the streets of London, then coming home to me when I will then contract syphilis like Catherine?' Her voice was getting louder.

James was struck dumb, where on earth were these thoughts coming from? The words sounded absurd; he would never do what she was suggesting. Then he saw the book she was holding, the grim, shocking history of London.

Seeing she was still sad about it all, he wished she could see London as he did. There were magnificent things to buy, amazing shops, wonderful imports. Certainly, the odour of the streets was not pleasant, and then there was the Thames, but if only Laura could see it from his point of view. In time everything would change for the better, she must know this, she was from the future. *Alas, the present*, he thought, *was not changing fast enough for my beloved.*

Laura continued, 'Apparently I have no say in whether I go to bed with you or not. Isn't it a crime if I refuse to satisfy my husband?' She threw the book forcefully onto a small table that held a floral arrangement. The vase of flowers fell to one side. James noticed the water dripping onto the rug.

'My love is not fleeting,' he said quietly, heading for the door.

He turned back and said, 'I would never ask you to sleep with me unless you wanted to. Just know, I would always respect your wishes, I give you my word.' He left the room.

James felt uncomfortable being so direct, it seemed shocking; however, he realised that people in the future probably were like that, and that was a good thing.

He did not, however, have the courage to stay and hear a further comment from Laura, and so he had walked away.

However, his fear of losing her grew as his anger rose within and he was unable to check it. He marched back and said, 'For goodness' sake, Laura, you are making me out to be some sort of obnoxious character, which, I assure you, I am not!' His voice echoed loudly around the room.

Laura sat down heavily; *I can't do this*, she thought.

He came to her and knelt before her, taking both her hands.

'I cannot stay,' she said almost as a whisper. She was greatly distressed.

'I love you and you love me; I know you do. There is nothing for it but to stay.' Then more forcefully he said, 'I forbid you to go!'

'Don't tell me what to do, I am a liberated woman!' She snatched her hands from him.

James sprang to his feet. 'Liberated? Trapped by your fear of life, your unpleasant thoughts, there is only one thing for it, I will come with you back to your world!'

'No, you can't, you will—'

'Oh yes, I forgot!' he said cynically, 'I will disintegrate and die! Well then, you must stay, I insist!'

Laura stood to leave the room, but he reached out and touched her arm. She stopped, they stared at each other. His large blue eyes were filled with pain. He tilted her chin up and kissed her ever so gently. She responded, regretful that she had been unkind. She did love him, deeply, but it was all-consuming, so passionate. Also, she didn't wish to live in this frightful era of inequality, disease and unfairness.

'I am trying to change society,' he said gently, and then he whispered, 'you are greatly needed by my side.' He touched her face lovingly. 'Please learn to trust me, I would actually die for you, I love you that much. Can't you see it?'

'I am afraid to stay here. I do love you, I do! But things here are—'

James felt slightly exasperated. 'I had hoped you would see that when you married me, I, as your husband, would have your best interests at heart. I will always protect what is mine.'

Laura came from a very different era. This explained

her fear. Could she ever commit to James with all that was weighing her down? She felt tears on her face.

'Laura, I cannot bear to see you cry.' He handed her one of his French lace handkerchiefs. She took it and dabbed at her eyes.

He grew concerned; he had spoken brutally, something he never did.

'Forgive me my harsh words,' he said, his face sad. He moved closer to her now.

'Forgive me,' she said, her tears beginning again.

He held her and moved her about as one would rock a baby to sleep. He was filled with such emotion, he feared it would be the undoing of him. Maybe he loved her too much, was that even possible?

'I think my place is here,' she said calmly, sincerely.

He pressed her to him, elated.

Eventually they sat together, James rejoicing in his luck.

'You know I don't think I will ever succeed with that maze.'

He smiled at her words.

Chapter 19

A PLEASANT SURPRISE

The following week, they had barely sat down to dinner, when Henry explained in a whisper to James that a gentleman had come to the Manor and wished to speak with him urgently.

Curious, James said, 'Pardon me, Laura,' and then went to the library where Pierre Jardin was waiting.

Pierre was an underweight, somewhat diminutive figure dressed in a wrinkled black jacket. He wore a white shirt with a bow at his neck, dark green breeches, grey stockings and black shoes. He held a three-point black hat in his hand and smiled, standing up and greeting James warmly.

'Bonsoir, monsieur,' he started.

James nodded cautiously.

He spoke in French, which James encouraged as he also spoke the language.

'I am Pierre, the husband of Franchette.'

James was stunned.

'How is the good lady?' he said in reply.

'I am afraid Franchette died two weeks ago, monsieur, from influenza.'

'My sympathies, sir.' James thought of the lovely woman Franchette had been, and a sadness tugged at his heart.

'The reason I have come,' Pierre started awkwardly, 'Franchette was my wife, and when we married, she was with child.' He looked uneasily at James.

'No matter,' encouraged James, smiling. He was rather religious and lived his life to a higher code of conduct than most; however, he tried to never be condescending of others who were not aristocrats, knowing full well his money set him apart from most of society and some of the misery bestowed on the less fortunate.

'She was expectant with your child, Sir James.'

James's eyes grew wide with astonishment.

'I begged her to tell you, however, she was very stubborn about it, and I was happy to have the boy call me Papa . But now, I feel his place is with his true father. I am a humble farmer, and he can have a much better life with you, if you are— how you say in English, agreeable?'

James suddenly smiled and gripped Pierre by the shoulders. 'That is so wonderful!' he exclaimed forcefully.

'Pierre, why didn't she let me know? I could have sent money.'

'She believed you did not want her, that you had thrown her away. It made me very sad; I believed otherwise, monsieur.'

'Yes, and you would have been right, I would have taken care of you, Franchette and the boy!' James deeply regretted that he had not sent for her, all because he had been wrapped up in his own life, his misery, while another dear person had needed him.

Pierre said, 'Perhaps it was her pride, she was a very stubborn girl.' He looked wistfully into the distance, his sadness apparent.

'Well,' said James, trying to steer the conversation elsewhere. 'What is the young chap's name?'

'Anthony. He is four years old now.'

'Anthony, I like that!'

Pierre showed great relief and smiled broadly.

James said he was willing to bring Anthony back to Paris to visit, but Pierre thought a clean break would be for the best. James nodded solemnly. 'Well,' he said 'if you change your mind and ever wish to see him, you only have to send word, and I shall definitely oblige! Where is Anthony?'

'I left him with your lady, Mrs Jones.'

'With Margaret, good, I am dying to meet him!'

They walked rather hurriedly to the kitchen, where Mrs Jones was feeding the child bread, butter and jam. The little blond-haired boy was drinking milk and looked up with large blue eyes, just like his father's. The two men then accompanied Mrs Jones and Anthony to a large bedroom where he was put to bed. Pierre was rather teary-eyed when he left the little one to sleep, and James walked with him to the front door.

As he left, Pierre said, 'Thank you, monsieur, you are a good man.'

'Wait,' James replied, 'do you need money, I can—'

'No, that is not necessary. I am very happy you will care for him, he is your son now.'

James waved at the carriage as it left the Manor and stood transfixed for a very long time, partly in happiness, partly in disbelief. Tears stung his eyes.

The next two weeks turned out to be the happiest days James had ever experienced.

One day in the Green Room, after breakfast, the child had called Laura 'Mama.' Surprised, James and Laura smiled at each other.

Laura took Anthony every morning down to the lake, so he could feed bread to the ducks.

James watched them from afar. I have a son, he thought,

and Laura is going to be my wife. He was filled with wonder. After the wedding, she will be in my bed. He looked into the distance, trying to stop the tingling in his groin. He sighed and closed his eyes.

'James?' Laura called to him and gave him a puzzled look, 'What is it?' she said.

'Nothing, my dear, nothing.' He smiled back at her, if only she knew of his sensual thoughts.

The three went for a short walk, Anthony running ahead and ripping flowers from their beds, then handing them to his new mama.

James was religious and wanted Laura to go to church with him. At first, she went to please him, then she grew to like the rituals. However, she was not as restrained as James who always felt obligated to "live a religious life". Laura saw life as a chance to try to be a good person rather than follow to the letter a set of rules.

The days were idyllic, and James felt so alive. He had been trying his hand at landscape painting and set up an easel in the gardens. 'I can paint,' he said seriously.

'No,' Laura smiled. She had seen his attempts.

'Don't you think?'

Laura burst out laughing.

He embraced her. 'Thanks for your encouragement,' he said laughing.

They kissed.

'You are so delightful, my dear.'

'I love you, James.'

He said, 'I love you too my darling, I love you very much.' Then added thoughtfully, 'You are not worried about living here with me?'

'I am, it is so different.'

'I know, but trust me, we will be very happy. You can return as often as you like to see the professor, so long as you always come back to me.'

Laura looked up at him. 'Everything is so — settled now, I don't think we will ever be anything but happy,' she said, emphasising the word 'but'. 'Anthony will learn English and I will learn French; our lives will be wonderful.'

James felt reassured, closed his eyes and smiled.

One evening before dinner, Henry informed his master that Laura had asked to borrow a razor. Henry had obliged believing that Sir James would not mind.

'Of course,' James said.

When Laura came to the Green Room and was seated by

him, she was wearing a light-blue dress with quite a lot of lace and beading across the top. She had changed for dinner, which pleased him as she didn't always make the effort. Not that he minded, believing that she thought changing for dinner was an unnecessary exercise.

He served her with chicken soup, and as they began the second course of roast turkey and vegetables, he said, 'Darling, you needed my razor?' He asked because he was curious.

'Yes, I knew you wouldn't mind.'

After a moment, he said, 'And what would you need it for?'

'I like smooth legs,' she said simply and smiled. The shaver was difficult to use but she had persevered, no longer would she have the luxury of a beauty salon where she could go for a quick leg wax and facial.

James was offering Laura more turkey from a porcelain platter and just managed to put the plate down, rather than drop it.

She had caught him by surprise with the unexpected answer. His imagination ran wild and he looked down at his plate, spearing some carrot and shoving it in his mouth.

He tried to regain composure as he had thought of her naked smooth legs. His body wanted her. Although it was a delightful agony, it was still an agony.

There were times when he thought of how making love

to her would be, resulting in a struggle to regain his serenity. Being in love with such a beautiful being made him the happiest he had ever been; he was often stunned at his luck. He loved her immensely and would patiently wait for their wedding night, it could not be any other way. He respected Laura more than any other living person.

Maybe he should go to church in the morning to regain his virtuous composure.

Chapter 20

A RETURN TO MELBOURNE

One morning at breakfast, Laura told James that she would have to go back and see the professor.

He looked up, alert. 'How long will you be gone?'

'Well,' she smiled, 'since I will be marrying you and living here permanently, I thought I would wind up all my affairs and then return.'

James nodded, 'So how long?'

She thought for a moment, 'Four or five days.'

'Alright,' he said, 'it must be done.'

She stood and went to him. Standing behind him, she put her hand reassuringly on his shoulder. 'I will probably never leave again, well, just to visit the professor around Christmas time.'

He smiled up at her, taking her hand and kissing it gently.

One evening Laura retired to her room. Once she was

alone, she went into deep transitional integration. When the white picket gate came into view, she opened it and hurried along the path, passing the garden and swimming pool. Then it was through the sliding doors and up the staircase. Opening her eyes with a start, Laura felt sad. She was home.

It was very quiet and lifeless. She had grown accustomed to Anthony's boundless energy and felt that he was her son, the connection between them real. It was only natural for a mother to miss her child, even though it was for a short time.

Laura called the professor.

They had sat together going through paperwork. The next day there was a meeting with a lawyer to transfer her money to the hospital, and then there was an appointment with an accountant.

She had cancelled her life insurance and paid all her bills. Many of her possessions were sent to charity, brought to the tip or in the case of sentimental items, stored at the professor's home. She had given him her house keys, explained how to disable the security system and handed him the name and number of her gardener. The house would be rented, and he was to get the rent. It was in payment for care of the house. It put her mind at ease that all would be well when she returned to her other life.

The professor was walking with a cane now although he

had not transitioned back to Harold. 'I should go, but I have been very busy.'

He had, however, managed to get a flight to London and successfully retrieve the stamps. 'I only had to take them to a stamp dealer, and they were offered online and snapped up. I don't know how someone can pay all that money for stamps, but I did get the money into my bank account, and since then the hospital extension has gone ahead in leaps and bounds!'

Laura was elated, then said, 'I wish I had been with you, but I know you forgive me.' She eyed him and smiled.

'I can only say that I am thrilled you have fallen in love. I wish you great happiness,' he said. 'Are you going to try some of this cake? I bought it especially for you.'

Laura nodded at his thoughtfulness. 'Professor, I hope you know I will come back at Christmas time, maybe even other times, it's just that I have to commit to 1765, I can't have one foot in here and then be toing and froing, you know?'

The professor shook his head, 'Yes, a clean break, eh?'

'I love James, and I must be with him.'

'I told you before, Laura, "love conquers all".'

'I don't know about that,' she laughed. 'Hey,' she said, excited, 'would you come visit me and James?'

The professor's eyes lit up, 'I don't see why not, what a great idea!'

They smiled at each other knowing that soon it would be time to part. Laura wished she could have him in her life every day, but it was just not possible.

They went together to see the work on the additions to the hospital. She knew in her heart that it all would be completed. Laura, for a fleeting moment, thought of Morley and Southeby. It warmed her heart that the professor as well as James, were people who cared enough to change society.

Chapter 21

AN ALARMING DIAGNOSIS

For her return to Harrington Manor, Laura chose to wear clothing more suited to that time as well as sturdy boots with low heels. She disliked the shoes available in London that James had offered to buy for her. It was exciting to be going home. She smiled. Home, yes, Harrington Manor is home.

Upon going into transitional integration, she arrived at the mansion. It had been snowing. Pulling her coat around her, thrilled to be back, she walked briskly to the front door.

In the grand hall, Nicholas was standing in the distance, as well as Henry, Jacob and Mrs Jones, who when she saw Laura, began to cry.

'What's wrong?' said Laura.

Nicholas came to her side, taking hold of both her hands. 'Laura, James is gravely ill. I do not think he can survive.'

Shocked, she pulled free and ran to the bedroom. James was propped up on pillows and Dr Stevenson had placed leeches on his bare chest. Another physician was assisting. One of the large glass-paned doors had crept open, and a crisp air was in the room.

James was pale, coughing and struggling to breathe.

She came to him, and anger filled her.

'Get those things off him!' she wailed.

Dr Stevenson said, 'What on earth are you saying, get out of here woman!'

Laura screamed Nicholas's name.

He ran to her.

'Get everybody out of this room, you know I can make him well. I need everyone gone!' she screamed the word 'gone' so loudly that Nicholas flinched.

He hesitated then nodded at the doctor, 'Please leave now, you have done all you can.'

The two doctors were shocked and gave Laura a disdainful look. 'You will not cure him, he has pneumonia!' said Dr Stevenson. His colleague scrambled to gather up his medical paraphernalia.

'Please,' said Nicholas.

They left, glaring at Laura.

She regained her composure and told Nicholas, 'You need

to gather the servants together, and inform them to do exactly as I say without question.'

'Alright,' he said and left the room.

Laura came to James, and upon seeing her he said, 'Laura, you need to go back, you mustn't be trapped here, I am dying and—'

'You're not dying, James. I will not allow it.'

She picked the slimy creatures off his chest.

She ran to the doors that opened out to the gardens and banged them shut. Hurrying from the room, she told Jacob to heat water for her and light a fire in the Oak Room. Next, servants were directed to remove all the rugs in the Oak Room and wash the floors with hot water and rum.

'Rum?' exclaimed Mrs Jones.

'It is the only thing I can think of that is a disinfectant.'

'A what?'

'Margaret, please.' Laura knew it was not ideal, but they did have rum, so this was a solution of sorts.

'Sorry, my lady,' and with that, Mrs Jones set to work.

Clean linen was put on the bed, and James was carried to the Oak Room. Laura would make this the sick room, as there were no doors to the gardens, and it seemed warmer.

She told Mrs Jones that bedding, when being washed, had to be boiled for forty-five minutes from now on.

The servants were unsure of all these directions but they obeyed.

Laura was slightly panicked she didn't know what to use to help James. There was nothing very much in the way of medical supplies or cleaning products. But she had been fascinated by an old herb book when she was a teenager. There had been a description of a water treatment and she closed her eyes, trying to remember the instructions.

Suddenly she dashed to the library and tried to find anything that could help. It took some time, however *The Complete Herbal* by a gentleman called Culpeper filled her with such relief, she sat down abruptly.

Rushing to the herb garden, she tried to find anything that could help. She studied the book.

Nicholas, who was still at the Manor, handed her his cup of tea. 'Here, you need this.'

She gulped it down, trying to regain some calm.

'Are you alright?' he said with concerned eyes.

She nodded, 'I know what to do, this book is a godsend. I just have to find the right herbs.'

Out of the corner of her eye, she saw it, vervain, growing profusely, crowding out the sage and parsley.

'I don't believe it!' she cried.

Nicholas looked confused.

James had a very high temperature; his lungs were in very bad condition. Laura subjected him to a continuous application of a cloth that had been soaked in tepid water; he was also given cold water to drink and received cold applications to his back.

After this relentless procedure, and after many hours had passed, he began to somewhat recover. He would at times feel chilled, and Laura would stop, putting a stocking filled with heated oatmeal on his torso.

The poultices made from different herbs found in the herb garden were applied to James's chest. The most effective being vervain, which was chopped into small pieces, boiled, then mixed with suet.

Three days after Laura had arrived back at the Manor, James seemed to settle. His breathing was almost normal.

'Laura,' he whispered.

She had been dozing in a chair by his side and jumped up, took hold of his hand, and smiled.

'How do you feel?' she asked

'I'm hungry.'

'That's what I wanted to hear.'

She began to cry; he squeezed her hand.

Laura had been insistent that anyone near James had to wash their hands with soap and hot water and were never to stand close to him. Also, at all times the Oak Room must be kept warm.

Although exhausted, she would sit nearby and watch over the patient, who had stopped coughing and seemed to sleep for hours. His breathing was still slightly laboured, but he was getting better. She did not wish to think otherwise.

She kept having a terrible thought. The professor, when they first met, explained many things about transitional integration. History could not be changed by an individual from another era. It just was not possible. Was saving James going to work? What if he was destined to die? It was most worrying.

She was insistent that her instructions be followed to the letter, and because of this, she was viewed as somewhat odd, even difficult.

One morning, Nicholas, who had come to visit, walked down the hall with Laura when she said, 'I'm sorry Nicholas, I don't mean to be disagreeable, I am just trying to help James. You know I come from another time.' She was aware James had confided in Nicholas about her and had sworn him to secrecy.

As well as Nicholas, James had informed Nigel, who did not impart Laura's secret to his wife, who was completely incapable of keeping secrets. This irritated him at times, while others found Jennifer amusing.

Nicholas moved closer to Laura. 'I was sworn to secrecy of the fact, I shall never divulge anything that would cause you concern. I understand you have knowledge that can save him, knowledge that we do not. Rest assured.'

Then he said, 'I tend not to look at the obstacles, rather the solutions. You are the solution. You can trust me.' Nicholas smiled at her.

Laura nodded, touching his arm.

She had the largest brown eyes he had ever encountered.

At her touch, he observed her face, her breasts, he took note of her figure. He noticed the tip of her black leather boots under her unfashionably slim skirt. He realised she could not possibly be wearing a petticoat and was, despite looking exhausted, a very attractive woman.

He had first encountered her at the Harrington Manor party, where Jennifer had introduced her as Mrs Laura Wesley, and Nicholas had been taken aback at the look of her. Unbeknown to her, she had outshone all the other ladies, with their exaggerated face paint and hair, who paraded smugly in their hoop petticoated dresses that made movement awkward. She was stunning, and he had felt his heart quicken in her presence. Then he had smartly moved away, should by chance James detect his admiration, which was carnal.

One day after lunch, while James was sleeping, Laura took a bath and then sat in the main bedchamber, which would become theirs after they married, she imagined, although, she had become aware that husbands and wives in 1765 had separate bedrooms. *How peculiar*, she thought.

Exhausted she barely managed to put on a nightgown and climbing into the huge bed, collapsed into a deep sleep.

She would religiously spend a very short time with Anthony each morning. Mrs Jones then taking over, bringing him to the lake to feed the ducks. Gerald would sometimes play games with the child in the gardens.

In the next two weeks, James recovered. He would sometimes be brought outside to sit in the garden and sip herbal tea. He was trying to become accustomed to the taste; strict orders from Laura were that he had to drink several cups of different infusions a day.

He began to look forward to her applying his poultices as they seemed to help. He still felt weak and would only walk very slowly.

Then, upon waking one morning, James felt stronger. He ordered Jacob to prepare a bath for him. After which he shaved and dressed, telling Henry that he wished to eat breakfast in the Green Room. James noted the pleased expression on the servant's face and touched him on the shoulder. 'I'm back Henry,' he said.

James, Laura and Anthony would take a walk together each morning. On one such occasion, James said, 'You saved my life, I can't believe it.' He put his arm around her waist and kissed the top of her head.

It was around this time that twenty-year-old Louise joined the servants of Harrington Manor. She spoke English with a French accent and was a most agreeable girl.

The refined features of her face would define her as pretty, rather than a beauty, with wispy light-brown curls. Anthony had liked her immediately. Laura had noticed that her clothing was worn and had obtained new attire for her as well as new shoes. The staff at Harrington Manor had been pleasantly surprised that Laura made sure they were well cared for. James was a kind man but sometimes missed seeing what servants needed.

She also could be seen wandering around their quarters by the kitchen and would peer into the larder, the gun room and the meat store, so as to become familiar with the running of the Manor. There was a new rule amongst the servants that Laura insisted everyone get acquainted with soap and hot water.

Chapter 22

A SAD OCCURRENCE

James left one morning by carriage to visit Nigel and Jennifer. Laura had declined to join him; she was tired and needed to relax.

A woman by the name of Agnes Jennings came to the Manor and begged to speak to Laura. The young lady had black hair that was piled high on her head with pearls attached. Her pale-blue eyes looked sad, and she was dressed in a very frilly, light-brown outfit with a grey cape and matching hat.

When the two women were in the main drawing room, Laura gestured for Agnes to sit down.

'Now, to what do I owe the pleasure of your visit?'

'It's Nicholas,' she said, 'he is ill, he asked that I fetch you, he said you could restore him to health.'

Laura knew that Lord Lawrence was a single man and was partial to the odd mistress. She suspected that Agnes was one of them, though it was unusual that she had come to Harrington Manor.

Laura said, 'Sick, how, what's wrong?'

Agnes shook her head; she had tears in her eyes.

'But surely Dr Stevenson saw to Nicholas?'

She shrugged. 'I think so, but he is still ill.'

Laura was hesitant; what if he has the plague or smallpox? She did not wish to be exposed to any of that. In fact, she was concerned just talking to Agnes who may have caught God knows what from Nicholas.

Later in the day, Laura asked for a driver and a footman to accompany her to Dr Stevenson, informing them to be ever vigilant in keeping her safe.

The doctor received her with suspicious eyes but imparted to her that Nicholas had contracted smallpox after a trip to London.

Laura brightened, feeling it was possible to do something to assist.

She would visit and speak to Nicholas, then commence herbal teas and poultices. She looked out the window of the carriage; what herbs were the best? She picked up Culpeper's book, which she had brought with her.

When she arrived at Hatherleigh Hall, she could not believe the size of it. It had many storeys and around twenty-five front windows of various sizes. The light-brown, brick mansion had an impressive entrance, making Laura feel small as she pulled at the bell, which rang out very loudly. How could these aristocrats have so much, and the poor so little?

A servant, who had a strong smell of tobacco about him, opened the door. He noticed Laura's footman and driver standing by the coach.

'I wish to see Lord Lawrence. I believe he is expecting me.' The servant was dressed in a grey coat, a cream colour shirt, light-cream breeches with matching stockings, and black shoes. He was a small man, about thirty years old. His brown hair was tied back with a black ribbon.

He bowed and let her pass into the hall. Upon closing the door, which echoed all the way through the mansion, he turned to her and said, 'I am very sorry, madam, His Lordship has died.'

Laura, upon her return to Harrington Manor, found James sitting in the gardens. He took time to recover from the unexpected news.

The funeral was an amazing affair. Nigel and Jennifer had rushed back from Edinburgh where they had been on holiday. There was no representation from the palace. George may not have approved of the lord's mistresses, or it may have been true that he was simply unable to attend. A few gentlemen had made the trip from Paris, and one rather tired man came all the way from Ireland. He was introduced as a dear friend.

When James and Laura returned to the Manor, they took afternoon tea in the gardens, where Anthony played a ball game with Gerald, the servant rather taken aback by the strenuous activity. Louise sat close by, ever vigilant. Peter the peacock approached Laura, who quickly gave him his usual afternoon treat of chopped carrots. James smiled.

Then he said pensively, 'I will have to ask Nigel to take care of everything should I pass away.' Since Nicholas had died, someone needed to be chosen as a replacement for the task.

Laura looked up at this unexpected remark.

'I believe he is trustworthy and would do the right thing by Anthony. Everything I have should pass to our son,' he said thoughtfully, 'and I trust Nigel to make sure you are well cared for.'

Laura said, 'You don't seem to have any relatives left.'

'I have lost all, now Nicholas is gone. Disease is a cruel thing.' It had been a great source of unhappiness for him.

'You do not have any relatives either,' he said reflectively.

'No, I grew up an orphan.'

'Do you know who your relatives were?'

She shook her head. 'I don't really think about it. Besides, I have you and Anthony now, don't I?'

'Absolutely!' he said, smiling.

After some thought, James said, 'We do good things, Laura. With you by my side we will accomplish a lot.'

'Always remember, James, I cannot change history, the professor told me never to believe I could.'

He nodded wisely. 'But you can advise me. Now with that, I can change things.' He then raised his eyebrows and smiled. Laura thought about this; it did make sense of sorts.

Chapter 23

A JOYOUS EVENT

On a beautiful sunny day, Laura married James.

Excitement filled the corridors of Harrington Manor.

James had gone to extraordinary lengths for his wedding apparel. His grey silk jacket and breeches were embroidered and bejewelled beyond all expectations. He even powdered his hair as was the fashion. His lace was the finest Paris could produce. He wore black shoes and a large ruby and silver pin at his neck.

Laura, on the other hand, had a dressmaker come to the Manor and rejected many of the ideas put to her, settling for a simple cream gown with minimal embroidery. The dressmaker sighed. What a strange one the soon-to-be Lady Harrington was. But it was not her place to reason why. She had heard amazing things of the work Sir James and Laura had done at Southeby Hall and Morley Place, tirelessly working for the poor and the sick. It was also said that Sir James was happier these days, his sadness had often worried everyone.

James did not want the ceremony to take place in the Harrington Manor chapel. Rather he fancied St Wilfrid's church in Alford, being fond of its simplicity. Some were surprised that he had selected this church, which could never boast of being grand. However, he had vowed to keep things simple knowing that his future wife could easily be overwhelmed by pomp and extravagance.

Laura was delighted when realising the ceremony would be modest. She had forfeited everything in her past life to commit to James.

She thought about her future husband, he was exquisite and when he spoke or was near, she felt the love in her whole being. It had nothing to do with his wealth, it was the man himself. He was everything good and true, and that was what she wanted. He was more than anything her previous life could offer.

Only a small number attended the actual ceremony. The bride, the groom and minister as well as Nigel, Jennifer, her two sisters, together with two business partners of Sir James.

King George was unable to attend, however, he sent his and

Queen Charlotte's best wishes. Laura would have felt anxious with the king at their wedding, so perhaps it was for the best.

James was also secretly pleased that there had been no gossip about Laura or Anthony. *Probably*, he thought with great delight, *because of the good things they did for the community.* He had stopped Hugh Williams with his venomous comments, and people were greatly relieved that Hugh no longer resided in the community. Willow Farm had been sold, and Hugh had quietly disappeared from Lincolnshire. Although Anthony could be seen as illegitimate, no negative whisperings occurred, and everyone looked lovingly towards the child.

Sixty people attended the festivities at Harrington Manor. Everyone smiled as Sir James seated himself in the Green Room with his wife at his side. Others then took their places at the large tables overflowing with food.

Laura was amazed that there were actually fifteen courses. Starting with soup, main dishes, side dishes and sweets. The meat dishes had to be placed in certain areas, and many things were all served at once. It all seemed very formal, yet to Laura's thinking it was unusual. She ate very little, ever mindful that she did not always know the correct etiquette. Everyone seemed to follow a code of polite behaviour that boarded on rigid, and she saw the dignified wedding guests as being very restrained. She knew that this was just the way people acted at banquets and celebrations.

Once the meal had concluded, a wonderful, aged wine, as well as port, flowed freely. Laura waited patiently and was served a cup of tea which she thoroughly enjoyed.

The new Lady Harrington delighted everyone when she danced with her husband, after which the guests joined in.

Later in the evening, James and Nigel, with drinks in hand, watched as an excited Jennifer escorted the bride around to meet the guests.

James took a sip of his port. 'I am very nervous, Laura will be in my bed this evening, she is now my wife,' he babbled.

'No need to be, old chap, you have been wanting to marry her since you first laid eyes on her. I know you are a religious man, however, one must endeavour to enjoy some happiness in life, what?'

James still looked uneasy. Nigel put a hand on his shoulder, smiling warmly. 'Well overdue for you, James.' Then as an afterthought he said, 'Perhaps you could tame her a little?'

'Tame her? She is mesmerising, intelligent, why would I want to tame a beautiful woman like that?' James was very excited.

Nigel, surprised, had no reply. He envied his friend. He loved his own wife, Jennifer, but she was rather frivolous. The truth of the matter was, theirs was not a passionate union.

He had not yet taken a mistress but knew it was inevitable.

Chapter 24

HAPPINESS

When all the guests had left, Laura went into the main bedchamber where she changed into a very simple white nightgown. She let her hair fall loose to her shoulders and smiled at herself in the large mirror.

Soft candlelight in the room gave a romantic atmosphere.

Later, James appeared in a light-brown, floor-length, embroidered dressing gown.

He was now calm and confident, and came very close, kissing her then lifting her into his arms and gently laying her on the bed.

'Laura, are you alright?' he said and smiled. She nodded.

He sat on the divan and removed all his clothing. He did not remove the black ribbon from his hair. Totally nude, he moved to the other side of the bed. Her heart quickened.

He knelt on the bed, towering above her. 'I don't believe

you married me today,' he smiled down at her.

'I did.'

'I am now your loving husband.'

'Yes,' she said softly. She felt excited.

'I will always love you, always take great care of you.'

'I know.'

He kissed her passionately. 'You aren't afraid of me, are you?'

'I could never be afraid of you.' She reached up and touched his face, then tucked a strand of his blond hair back in place.

He took a firm hold of her; his hands began to roam over her body, exciting her like no other before him.

Chapter 25

TOGETHERNESS

James hardly slept. Gratitude kept him awake that this angelic creature loved him. His love for her was overwhelming.

His beautiful Laura was willing, accommodating. It was amazing; a wife who moved her body in unison to his. She made him feel on fire, clinging to him so forcefully, so that his heart raced. He had fallen back spent, totally mesmerised by this love that was so deep.

Now he lay on his back, with Laura sleeping at his side. Her bent knees touching his; her long fingers on his bare chest. He could just make out in the dim light, the wedding ring on her finger. It filled him with happiness. *She really is mine*, he thought.

His hand touched her soft body. He grew aroused. Now awake, she slid her fingers down him. He could hardly breathe for the delight he felt. She pulled him to her, kissing him.

He had had few sexual encounters, finding that women seemed to endure rather than enjoy them. Even Franchette.

Were other men fortunate enough to have a spouse like mine? He thought. *She is very loving, almost unbelievably so.*

Some time passed, and he glanced at his lovely wife; her eyes were closed. He lay beside her quietly reflecting on how happy he was.

When the morning light began to creep further into the room, Laura stirred. He stared at her, and she at him. After a while she said, 'I love you.'

'Amen to that.' He grinned.

In the coming weeks, he was still mesmerised by her. It thrilled James how at times when he was seated, she would come from behind and put her hand on his shoulder, touching him in a very loving way. No one ever had made him feel so special. This beautiful creature truly loved him.

The way she would smile at him from across a room. Or smile and nod at him from very far away. He was so in love with her, he feared it may cease at any moment. How could he survive without this amazing love? It would finish him should he ever lose her. Then he would reassure himself. *She's mine, she will always be mine.*

One evening after they had made love, he asked, 'Will you always love me?'

She looked at him. 'Yes.'

'Promise?'

'Promise. I love you very much, James,' she said softly, her eyes sincere.

That was all he needed to hear. He thought back to when she had left and returned to Melbourne, he was shocked at the emptiness that had engulfed him. Absence had been a horrid word at that time. He suddenly had empathy for Hugh, realising how one could succumb to the perils of alcohol over the loss of love.

Laura did not leave the bedroom after they made love. She preferred to stay with him all night. It was not common, but he was pleased. Perhaps in the time Laura came from, it was normal for a husband to enjoy his wife's company all night.

One morning, after her bath, Laura had dressed and stood at the big mirror. James came behind her and put his hands on her shoulders.

'Beautiful,' he said, looking at her reflection.

'A woman has more to offer than just beauty.'

He raised his eyebrows, 'I know that.'

She was concerned at how the only thing of value a woman appeared to have in this era was beauty. But to be fair, James often remarked on her intelligence and her common sense, even though he would also often comment on how beautiful his wife was.

'I'm just Laura,' she said.

'A very beautiful Laura.'

She sighed.

'And a very intelligent one to boot.' He smiled playfully.

'James, I'm going to grow old!' she stated firmly.

He squeezed her tightly, 'And I am going to grow old with you!' he said enthusiastically.

They both laughed.

Laura suddenly took the black ribbon from James's hair, which fell freely, framing his face. He touched it awkwardly wondering why she had done this. She was being mischievous and grinned up at him. He always had his hair tied back, even when he went to bed.

'You look like a rock star,' she smiled.

'A what?'

'Never mind, you look very handsome.'

He kissed her lips gently. She liked that, his gentleness, his caring eyes.

She put her hand on his shoulder and he sat down. Then Laura brushed his hair and put the ribbon back in place.

Smiling, he said, 'I didn't think I could ever be this happy.'

Chapter 26

AN INHERITANCE

Later that day, James was sitting in the library at his writing desk. He was mulling over paperwork and looked rather sad. His thoughts were of Nicholas; he wished there had been more time to spend with his only surviving relative, but now he was gone.

As Laura came into the library, she noticed his demeanour. 'James, is something wrong?'

'I have inherited Hatherleigh Hall.'

Knowing how large it was, she asked, 'Are you going to keep it?'

James looked towards her and smiled.

'What?'

'I thought I could turn it into a hospital for the poor, it would be better than Southeby Hall. Then Southeby could become like Morley Place, that way I could help more unfortunate souls.'

'That is wonderful, but you will need to persuade the Lincolnshire doctors, will they agree to help you?'

James took hold of her hand. 'I know you are not swayed, or influenced by money my dear, however, the rest of the world is. I am sure for the right sum I can encourage the unwilling to join us in this venture.'

'You are amazing,' she said.

'If that be true, it is because of my supportive wife. Cup of tea?'

Chapter 27

A TRIP TO THE BEACH

On a fine day in June, the Harringtons and their good friends Nigel and Jennifer went to the beach on the Lincolnshire coast for a picnic. Laura shielded her face from the sun with an umbrella. She wore a cream-coloured dress, simple and attractive, while Jennifer was in a bright yellow dress, with a train behind, which quickly became soiled. Laura never could grasp how this fashion was in place, it was not practical.

Louise busied herself setting up blankets and arranging baskets of bread, bottles of wine, platters of cold sliced meats, fruits and cakes, as well as dishes, glasses and cutlery, with Gerald gladly helping her. Anthony sat down nearby, and she handed him a piece of cheese.

James was deep in conversation about Hatherleigh, Nigel listening intently. Jennifer and Laura looked out to the coastline where the view was remarkable, birds flew overhead and there was a large vessel out at sea, its sails flapping in the breeze.

Anthony dashed away and ran along the beach, picking up shells.

It was a wonderful day with fine weather.

Some time had passed when suddenly Louise screamed, seeing Anthony floating face down in the ocean.

Laura turned and in horror raced to take hold of him. Dragging him from the sea and laying him flat, she started to perform resuscitation. She tilted his head back and pinched his nose, putting two breaths into him, then thirty compressions on his chest, and quickly repeating the procedure.

James stood up in shock, his knees weak. Nigel and Jennifer were rooted to the spot.

'What is she doing?' said Jennifer, frowning.

'She knows things we do not,' James managed.

After agonising minutes passed, Anthony coughed. Laura pulled him into a sitting position and tapped hard on his back.

He complained in a very small voice.

Laura roughly pulled him to his feet.

'Anthony, are you alright?'

He nodded.

'Anthony, tell Mama you are alright!'

He responded in French. 'Oui,' he said and reached up for her.

She took him into her arms and came to James, nodding at him.

Everyone touched the child and was greatly relieved. The moment was solemn until James said, 'I think we should all return to the Manor and have a cup of tea.'

Despite herself, Laura laughed, and upon seeing that, everyone else did. James always thought a cup of tea would fix everything, why would this dire occasion be any different?

Anthony clung to Laura, and she kissed him. They were both very wet. He was alright, he would forget this day, as hopefully they all would.

Upon returning to the Manor, Laura bathed the child, who would laugh splashing the water about and talk to her, some words in English. She was amazed how he had bounced back from his encounter with death.

When she put him to bed, James came to her and put his arm around her waist. He looked grim, his large blue eyes sad. He did not speak but eventually smiled at her.

As Anthony closed his eyes, the candles were extinguished with their pungent smoke dancing through the air. The door was gently closed, and Laura walked down the long hall,

James holding her close. A disaster had befallen them, but they had triumphed. However, it would take some time for recovery; this event had shaken James to the core.

The next morning Laura and James were in the Green Room, they had just finished breakfast.

Louise came and stood before them.

'You wanted to see me, sir?'

James put down his cup of tea. 'I find your lack of care yesterday almost unforgivable. I charged you with the care of our son, and you let us down.'

Louise became very distressed, 'I am sorry, sir.' She wrung her hands.

He stared at her. He felt anger but dismissed her by raising his hand in the air. He thought maybe tomorrow he would be calm and could explain that her services were no longer required. He felt so betrayed.

She ran from the room; her sobs could be heard all the way down the hall.

After a while he looked at Laura, 'She will have to go,' he said. He felt more composed.

'Please reconsider.'

He was shocked at her words.

'Louise was to look after Anthony and look what happened!' His voice was harsh.

'We are the parents,' Laura simply said, seeing the incident as an unfortunate mishap. 'No one had been watching Anthony.'

He looked at her then thought about it. 'Um,' he said begrudgingly.

'Well just think about it, everyone makes mistakes, it was an accident.'

She kissed his cheek. He reached for her, but she was too far away now, heading for the door.

Laura turned and said, 'I'm just going to speak to Mrs Jones.' She smiled and left, closing the doors behind her.

James rubbed his forehead; Laura had planted doubt.

The next day, after discussions with James, Laura went to see Louise.

'I am sorry, Lady Harrington, I—'

'It's alright. We all are to blame to some extent, no one was watching.' She took the girl's hands into hers. Louise was struck by Lady Harrington's kindness.

As the renovation of Hatherleigh Hall would be extensive, Laura said, 'Sir James and I will be extremely busy over the coming months. I need you to always watch over our son and take great care of him.'

Louise was shocked, she thought she would be sent back to Paris.

'Oui— oui, I will, I promise!' she said eagerly, dropping to her knees.

Laura bent down, taking her into her arms.

'Mets ça derrière toi, Louise.' Louise was touched at the French words saying that she should put this behind her.

To further encourage the girl, Laura said, 'It's alright, I spoke to Sir James, all is forgiven. Let's go for a walk in the gardens.' At that, Louise brightened.

James had agreed to allow the young woman to stay, greatly guided by Laura's view that it was an accident, and anyway, no one had kept an eye on Anthony. *Perhaps we were all to blame*, he thought.

He was sitting in the drawing room when he noticed Laura and Louise walking in the gardens. Presently Mrs Jones came out with Anthony at her side. He ran to his mother, and Laura took hold of his hand.

James smiled; all was well. The little boy, who looked just like his father, was very clever. James absolutely adored him and would take him riding on Captain and for walks in the gardens, where they spoke French.

He thought fondly of Franchette, who had given him his precious son. Then as always, his thoughts turned to the one who had his heart. Laura had brought a calmness to his mind and great happiness to his life.

Chapter 28

THE ART GALLERY

In Oxford, at the Christ Church Picture Gallery, Christopher and Lisa ran indoors, escaping the heavy rain, all smiles and energy. He shook his wet brown hair. He was tall and handsome. Lisa, who was a petite blonde, slid her phone into her pocket, then bunched her hair up with an elastic band.

'So where are these portraits of your relatives?' she asked, slightly breathless.

Chris looked at his program, smoothing out the wet pages. 'Um, section seventeen,' he read aloud, 'depicts typical portraits of the era 1760 to 1789.'

When they came across the two paintings, Lisa was amazed.

'Wow, these are your relatives?'

Chris Harrington nodded. 'Well yeah, but long ago.'

'Look, Lady Harrington is smiling' said Lisa, delighted.

'Those,' she waved her hand around at the other portraits in the section, 'not so much.' Looking at the other portrait, she said, 'Even Sir James is smiling, they both look happy.'

'They lived a long life, they were happy, did a lot of good for the community,' Chris said, rather proud.

'How many children did they have?'

'One, Sir Anthony Harrington, curious for that time, when there was no contraception.' He nudged her; Lisa laughed.

He looked at his watch. 'There's another art gallery I want to go to. There's a David Hockney on display. I want to see it.'

'Does he paint portraits too?' she asked.

'Swimming pools.'

'What?'

'Come on,' he smiled, 'I'll show you.' He took hold of her hand.

Chapter 29

PAINTING OF THE PORTRAITS

In September 1768, two artists were greatly engrossed in individual portraits of the Harringtons.

James turned to Laura, 'I think we need a break, my dear.'

Laura nodded and said, 'I shall get Mrs Jones to bring you afternoon tea, gentlemen.'

'Thank you,' the artists said, almost in unison.

James stretched out his arm to her, and they walked down the long hall leading to the Green Room.

He stopped at a huge painting that hung in an ornate frame.

'Our happy family,' he said.

The portrait was of James standing behind Laura, who was seated, with Anthony playing with toys at her feet. It had been completed after their wedding, a gift from James to his wife.

Laura smiled.

James said, 'I hope Mrs Jones has made some buttermilk scones for me.'

'You know she has.'

As they entered the Green Room, Anthony looked up. 'Mama!' he cried, delighted to see Laura.

Sitting alongside Anthony was King George drinking a cup of tea. He observed Laura and smiled.

Laura responded with a curtsy and grinned back at the king.

The visit was totally unexpected. James bowed and said, 'So good to see you again, sir.'

James then pulled out a chair and gestured for his wife to sit down, Anthony rushed to Laura, and she placed him on her lap.

Just then Mrs Jones set a plate piled high with buttermilk scones in the centre of the table.

THE END

9 781922 958358